Children of the Diadems

Sonia Braithwaite

Book One

In the Beginning

First published by Author House 9/12/2008

Revised by Sonia Braithwaite. 21/04/2012

Book cover illustrated by Matthew Willis

ISBN: 9780957274006

Dedication:

To my son Kane, my son Carl, and his pet cat, Clovis.
To my daughter Amanda Anara, and my granddaughters,
Gaia and Eden.
To Jack on the Island, who gave Carl the kitten.
To Carl's friends, Craig, Nikhil and Luke.

Introduction

When a sixth kitten is born unexpectedly to Tom's cat, Hildegarde, it is weak and may not survive.

Two of the children, Carl and his sister Gula, really want a kitten, and need to persuade their parents to let them have one of Hildegarde's kittens. But their mother Eleanor is reluctant, as she has had a terrifying experience with a creature she fears was a vicious cat.

Tom shares his anxiety in class about the sixth kitten.

The class teacher, Mrs Townsend, tells the children how important cats were in Ancient Egypt, and relates to them the myth about the Egyptian Goddess Bastet.

Later that evening the vet, Mr Hixson, has his doubts as to whether the sixth kitten will live. Carl's family visit Tom's home to see the kittens. Whilst they are there, a miraculous event takes place.

The Children learn that the sixth kitten may not be an ordinary cat after all. They were also told of a special quest, which they must fulfil. However, evil forces start to oppose them. Fortunately, they are helped along the way by Bastet, the Egyptian Goddess, and others on the side of good.

Chapter One

The Encounter

The sun had not long set, but the evening had grown dark quickly. Eleanor McKenzie, who was just three months pregnant, was returning from her usual evening walk. Just as she reached the tree at the entrance to the gravel pathway leading to her home, she noticed that the overhung branches had cast dark shadows across the path, in the shape of a horned figure. At first it made her smile. But then, as she paused to secure the buttons on her cream maternity coat, she heard a snapping of twigs. As she reached up to rearrange the shawl she had used to ward off the cold evening breeze, she received the fright of her life. A figure, clothed in black from head to toe, suddenly jumped down from the tree in front of her. It was making the most haunting sounds Eleanor had ever heard.

Eleanor screamed, half-expecting the figure to attack her, but it scampered off. She watched it run along the path. Its arms were outstretched and its black cloak was blown upwards by the wind. From the back it looked like

1

a giant bat. As Eleanor calmed down, she reasoned that bats don't run on two legs like humans.

Eleanor's scream had alerted her husband Phillip, who didn't like her walking alone at night. He was seated on their front porch, anxiously awaiting her return and rushed to her aid.

Once Eleanor explained how the mysterious figure had frightened her, he scolded her.

"This is the last time you go out alone at night, Eleanor. I know you enjoy these regular solitary walks, but you shouldn't go in your condition. The next time I'm coming with you."

Eleanor was shaken up so Phillip called the doctor.

"You are a strong young woman Eleanor McKenzie, just like your late mother, God rest her soul," said the doctor.

Eleanor was stretched out on the couch in the living room.

"You will be as right as rain in a day or so. Phillip, make sure she gets plenty of rest for a day or two, and I mean *rest* young woman," he said, smiling down at his patient.

"I will see to it that she has plenty of rest. I can assure you of that doctor," said Phillip.

Doctor Malcolm was seventy years old. He had given up general practice at fifty and had set up his own little private practice. He had not retired at sixty five, his licence was extended, which allowed him to continue practising. He was a tall, strong, pleasant looking man for his years.

As Eleanor looked up at him, she smiled saying, "Thank you doctor."

She noticed then how silvery white his partly receding hair had become; she could not see a strand of the shiny black hair he once had. He had been her family doctor for many years, her parents and grandparents had been his patients.

"If I were you I would report this incident to the police right away, Phillip."

"That I will do doctor," Phillip replied, with a serious expression. "Only a deranged person would pull a prank like that."

"Well, try not to let it spoil the rest of your evening. I'd better be off as I have another call to make."

"No rest for the good, eh doctor?" Phillip joked.

"Is that what they say?" the doctor asked, with a chuckle.

3

Before he shut the front door, Phillip watched as Doctor Malcolm got safely into his car and drove off.

After that incident, Phillip and Eleanor enjoyed frequent evening walks together, and had even talked and joked about her first experience, until it was practically forgotten.

She was in the sixth month of her pregnancy when she took a leisurely walk alone.

She had walked for about a mile until she came to the only three shops in the village, a newsagent, a butcher shop, and a small grocery; they were all closed.

She sat on the long red seat under the bus shelter, to have what she felt was a well earned rest.

Two other people had joined her, a young looking woman and a tall slim man. She could not guess the man's age because his head was bent; not once did he look up, not even when Eleanor shuffled to one end of the seat to create space for them to sit. The woman sat at the other end of the bench. The man had walked over to the butcher's shop and stood under the canopy, with his back to them.

"A lovely evening," said Eleanor to the woman who had looked at her stomach and smiled.

The woman nodded, "It's dusky," she replied, "Before we know it, it will be dark. That's the trouble with this village," she continued, "it always grows dark early, quicker than anywhere else I've been." She looked at Eleanor's stomach again. Eleanor smiled and instinctively cradled her bulging belly.

"Your first?" The woman asked.

"Yes," replied Eleanor, pleasantly, but couldn't help noticing how quickly the smile had vanished from the woman's face, and in place was a kind of hardness to her youthful, attractive looking features. It caused Eleanor to shiver, and for a moment or two she felt icy inside, even though it was a summer's evening.

A bus came, the woman got on, but the man didn't. Eleanor looked towards the spot where the man had stood, but he was gone. She sighed contentedly, dismissing him from her thoughts, then got up to start her journey back home, when Phillip rang.

"You shouldn't be walking home so late in your pregnancy, Eleanor," he said. "The baby is due in three months."

"I'll be just fine. You worry too much that's your trouble," was Eleanor's calm response.

"Someone has to do the worrying," continued Phillip. "You should be in the comfort of our home, resting, putting your feet up, not out walking in this hot weather, and by yourself again," he grumbled.

"Please stop fussing," said Eleanor. "I will enjoy the walk, and I'll be home sooner than you think. I can still move pretty fast even for a pregnant woman expecting a baby girl." Eleanor giggled playfully, to try and change Phillip's mood.

"And just how do you know that we are having a little girl?" Phillip asked, sounding happier.

Eleanor could tell that her husband was smiling.

"Oh, call it a woman's intuition," she replied pleasantly, and they laughed together.

"Well. Okay," Phillip agreed. "But hurry home before it gets dark."

As Eleanor walked on, she felt comforted from the memory of her husband's soft caring voice. She appeared oblivious of the fact that the evening was slowly becoming darker, until she looked up and realised that the street lights were all lit up. She looked at her watch, "My, it's 9:30 already," she said.

She was half way home when she stopped at the traffic lights, and stood waiting for the lights to change. She sniffed airily at the silence. She had not walked home alone for months, and she never had a problem with being followed. She had convinced her husband to trust and to believe that there was no danger for her walking home.

At the pace she was going, she felt that in 17 minutes she would be indoors; she had begun to hum softly and contentedly to herself. Suddenly, an incomprehensible feeling that she was being followed, took hold of her. It was so strong that she began to wish she had accepted her husband's offer and had waited for him.

She wasn't wrong, as she turned around, she noticed that she wasn't alone, and immediately she felt afraid. She could not make out for certain who or what she was seeing, because of the distance between them, but from the shape, she assumed that it was the figure of a woman.

Instantly her mind wandered back to the young woman she had met earlier at the bus stop.

"But why would she be following me? She took the bus," Eleanor whispered.

As she looked again, all she could make out was a kind of darkness within darkness, as flashes of the creature that had frightened her earlier on in her pregnancy returned; the fear which she felt at the time crept back inside her head and unnerved her.

Convinced that she was being chased by the cloaked fiend, she turned and began to take quick strides along the road, which now seemed endless to her. She knew that in her condition, it would not be possible for her to out-walk anyone, and her legs were beginning to feel a little heavy.

She reached a dimly lit street light, stopped and rested her body against the tall stone light pole, and tried to measure the distance between her and her pursuer, only to realise that the figure was larger than she had first thought, and it appeared to be crouched and ill-shaped.

"That is not the shape of a human being," she said, "Unless it has some kind of deformity. The growing darkness must be playing tricks with my eyes," she decided, rubbing them with shaky hands as she set off again. She was walking even faster than before, and within a few minutes she grew tired and stopped again, panting.

She looked behind her and saw that the creature was much closer than she had hoped it would be, and that it was down on all fours; her fear heightened.

"Good grief," said Eleanor, "It's inhuman, it's an animal." She stared even harder, "What sort of creature could be so large?" she asked herself.

She tried to walk faster, but the shape was moving quickly. She glanced again over her shoulder. This time, the figure no longer appeared to be a large animal, but a person walking with a stoop. She thought the person must be old, but the figure was moving so fast, gaining ground on her all the time, so she tried to walk even faster.

As the creature became visible, Eleanor saw to her horror that its human features were distorted. She wanted to run, but knew she could not. She felt the urge to turn around again, but she knew the thing behind her was unlike anyone she had seen before. She was about three hundred yards from her house now, but the creature was getting closer and closer.

Finally, she glanced to see that the creature was no longer walking on two feet; it was trotting on all fours. An overwhelming fear took hold of her.

9

"Oh my goodness, it's not a person," said Eleanor out loud.

The creature heard her. It began to snarl and to make hissing sounds. She froze on the spot with fear. "Oh my God," she whispered, "it sounds like a beast of some kind. Mother Mary, help me, I think it's after me!"

Somehow, Eleanor found the inner strength to start running as fast as her legs could carry her. She no longer cared to know who or what it was. All she felt was fear for her life and for the life of her unborn child.

She wanted to get away as quickly as possible, to reach home before it got to her. As Eleanor gained speed, so the creature behind her gained speed. She glanced behind again, long enough to decide that it was an animal after all.

"This thing can't be ordinary," she continued in a soft voice. "It looks like a prehistoric animal, or perhaps an experiment that went wrong."

Each time she whispered to herself, it growled, sounding more like a dog. It was menacing, but to Eleanor, even more alarming, was the fact that the creature became whatever image she had formed in her thoughts.

"Mercy me," cried Eleanor, losing courage. "What does it want with me? Deliver me from evil, my God," she cried again looking up, as she stubbed her left big toe. "If I stop, it could devour me. I am sure that is what it wants to do. Why else would it be chasing me?"

Eleanor became frantic. She was breathing with great difficulty and caressing the bump in her belly as she half-stumbled down the pavement.

Desperate, knowing she could not reach home before the creature trapped her, she ran towards the nearest house, but when she reached the gate it wouldn't open.

She was fleeing from a monster, and for all she knew, from the very jaws of death, but no one seemed to see her.

"Heaven help me!" she exclaimed. Remembering she had a mobile phone, she reached inside her coat pocket for it, but it was gone.

She attempted to scramble over the low garden wall that led to the front door of the house. Suddenly she slipped. One foot was on the wall and the other was still on the ground. She felt a sudden sharp pain up the back of her left leg, but she didn't stop. How could she, when she felt certain that she had to flee for her life?

"Angels, beings of love and light, I call to you," she cried. "Whatever it is, please don't allow it to catch up with me or hurt me."

She was in the grip of fear and dread as she looked behind again. The animal was still gaining on her and she was trembling.

"It's a demon, straight from hell itself. It wants to attack me," Eleanor cried, "but I won't let it." She became angry.

Knowing she had to protect the child in her belly gave her the courage to transcend her own fears. "You won't catch me," she yelled, "beast or no beast, demon or no demon."

In a moment or two, which seemed like forever, Eleanor had turned the corner and was near her house. She ran gasping straight through the open back gate and along the pathway; tall green shrubs had grown, which created a border on either side leading up to the gate of their back garden.

"Help me! Phillip, help me!" she yelled.

Phillip was in the garden outside and could hear nothing above the din of the music he had turned right up.

Eleanor was exhausted and could run no farther. She accepted her fate and waited. As she paused in her bewildered, almost collapsed state, a great purple ray of light beamed down from the sky and surrounded her like a force field.

She opened her mouth to scream, but nothing came out. She pushed with whatever little strength she had left inside her, but could not break free. She knew then that whatever surrounded her was impossible to penetrate because, the more she pushed the more it expanded, but she could see through it.

Eleanor stood and witnessed a huge black and white cat, transformed into what appeared to be a human shape, then into a large dark shadow; it encircled the purple shield around her. She could no longer see outside, but she heard the menacing sounds the frightening shape-shifting creature made.

The shadowy creature became distorted, and as it wriggled, two large white hands came out of it and pushed against the shield. The hands were immediately scorched, and the creature yelled as if in torture. From its large mouth came a howl like a dingo, being ripped apart by a far greater force.

Able to see through the shield once more, Eleanor watched open-mouthed as the shadow turned into the black and white cat again then transformed into the dense dark shadow, before it vanished out of sight.

"Thank you God," said Eleanor, in a soft mournful voice, as the force field released her. She watched it ascend into the sky and disappear into the clouds above. "It was a protective shield," she whispered.

She turned to run. On the pavement by the back gate, where the something or someone evil had been, she saw a faded red rose...

"Holy Moses!" cried Eleanor, and with all the strength she could muster, she yelled for her husband. She dashed into the back garden. Her face was contorted with fear and she collapsed right into Phillip's arms. "Something shielded me, from..." she managed to say just before she fainted.

Phillip lifted his wife up in his arms, hurried into the house and sat her down on the sofa. Above the sound of the music in their living room, Phillip heard the shrieks of something dreadful in the distance.

He turned off the stereo and ran upstairs to the bathroom to find the smelling salts. When he returned, he placed the small bottle close to Eleanor's nostrils, and the strong smell revived her.

"Phillip," she gasped, her voice shaking. She looked as though she had visited hell itself and had stared into the face of death. Her voice was low as she spoke.

"I have heard that there are creatures that walk in darkness and destructive spirits wandering about at noonday, but I never believed it, not until now," she told her husband, who held her hand as she rested her head on his shoulder.

"I should call Doctor Malcolm and let him take a look at you," he said. Eleanor did not reply. She carried on talking as if she hadn't heard what Phillip said.

"I have just had an encounter with one. I have just been attacked," she said, "by a vicious demon devil of a tomcat, straight from hell."

"What do you mean you have just been attacked? I had better call the police," he suggested.

"No, please, don't do that. They won't believe me," she said, still speaking softly. "Please call the doctor, Phillip. He will do."

"Eleanor, what really happened to you?" asked Phillip with a concerned look, clearly disbelieving her story.

"No creature living on earth could look as horrifying as that cat," was her response.

Eleanor looked into her husband's face and saw he had become as frightened as she was.

"Eleanor, are you saying that a cat chased you?"

Phillip's scared look left him and he looked flabbergasted.

"Look," she said, lifting up the skirt of her dress to reveal a long scratch above her ankle.

"Dear me!" cried Phillip. "How did you manage to get that? Did the cat scratch you?"

"No. I got it trying to jump over the garden wall, to get to the front door of a house. There was a thorn bush. I didn't notice that I had caught my foot on it until I felt the pain."

"Here, let me see to that," said Phillip. He got up, wet a clean cloth with cold water and dabbed the scratch. "Is that feeling any better?" he asked.

"It stings a little," she replied, "but I'll be okay. What's a little scratch compared with what I have just been through?"

"I cannot begin to imagine," replied Phillip.

"That hideous monster just caused me to put my life, and that of our unborn child, at risk. I tell you, what I saw was no ordinary cat."

"Okay, Eleanor," said Phillip, "I am thankful that you didn't come to any further harm."

Eleanor did not respond for a few moments, then she said,

"It *was* a demon, Phillip."

"You are safe now my love, you are home. Nothing or no one can come in here and hurt you, not while I am here." Phillip tried his best to comfort his wife. "You had better go and lie down," he continued. "Would you like me to carry you? You need to rest."

"You, carry me?" asked Eleanor.

"It certainly looks as though you have been through quite an ordeal," said Phillip, sympathetically.

"I'll do that, Phillip. In a little while I'll go and lie down. I just need to sit here a bit longer, but I could do with a drink of water. I am burning up inside," she told him.

Phillip wiped sweat and tears from his wife's face and dried her eyes. He went to the fridge and poured her a glass of water. At that moment he felt like crying with her.

That is how the story began.

Three months later, Eleanor gave birth to a beautiful baby girl. The couple had chosen to name the child Sara Elizabeth, after their mothers, but the moment they looked at the baby, the name Gula, escaped their lips at the same time.

The baby came into the world with the same mark as the one Eleanor had sustained on that dreadful day, in the same place on the back of her left leg, just above her ankle.

It was a day Eleanor would never forget. Her fear of cats grew worse every year, but especially on the anniversary of her ordeal.

Chapter Two

A New Day

Seven years went by. Eleanor and her husband Phillip, lived a happy and undisturbed life, and during that time, Eleanor had given birth to another child, a son. They had ignored the name 'Wobniar,' which came to their minds at the same time, instantly the baby boy was born, and instead they named him, 'Carl.'

"I prefer the name Carl," Phillip had decided, dismissing the other name, as he hugged and kissed his wife. "It means our beloved son will always be a free man," he told Eleanor that day, beaming with pride.

Autumn was not only Gula's favourite season of the year, it was nearing the end of November, and it was her birthday. The morning was cold but dry. Phillip and Eleanor had decided to begin their day with an early morning walk, while the house was being specially prepared for Gula's birthday party. They hadn't walked very far when they saw an old woman bending over and picking up dried twigs that had fallen off the nearby trees.

Phillip hurried over to her.

"Let me help you with that, old lady," he said, taking the sticks from her and tying the thick gold cord that she handed him around the bundle, in order to secure it.

The old woman sat down on a small patch of grass by the roadside and Phillip placed the bundle of sticks beside her. She was not dressed for the time of year. She wore a dirty old raincoat that had faded and looked as though it had seen better days. On her feet were pale brown plaited summer sandals. Her head was veiled with a large purple and gold scarf, which extended down to cover the back of her tatty coat.

As Eleanor and the children reached them, the old woman smiled.

"Hello," she said.

"Hello," said Eleanor.

"And what are your names?" she asked, looking at the children with interest.

"I am Gula, and this is my brother, Carl."

"Carl," repeated the old woman, a little mystified, but then she smiled at the children.

"Where is your home, and what are you doing sitting out here in the cold?" asked Eleanor, politely.

"I am a wanderer, by decree of the Ancient Gods and Goddesses," the old woman replied.

"Is that so?" asked Phillip, looking dubious.

"I can see that you don't believe me," said the old woman, looking straight into Phillip's eyes. "You find it hard to believe a lot of things, until you receive concrete proof."

"The cold has obviously got to you, old woman. If you live nearby, we can walk you home," said Phillip.

"And I will carry her sticks," said Gula.

Thinking the old lady was not quite in her right mind, Phillip spoke rudely about her out loud.

"This is how it often is with old people, at least sometimes. Their minds begin to lapse and play tricks on them," he said. "As a result, the memory is not like it used to be. Let's go, she won't be interested in anything we have to say to her, not really."

"And just how did you reach that conclusion, having never met me before?" asked the old woman, looking sad.

"All I have to say to you Phillip, is, I just can't leave her alone out here like this. The poor lady will freeze to death!" said Eleanor.

"And whose fault would that be?" Phillip asked, "Suppose we hadn't come along?"

"But, we are here dad," interrupted Gula. She turned to her mother. "We must help her, mummy."

"I know we must, Gula," replied Eleanor, giving Phillip one of her disapproving looks.

"If we leave her out in the cold, she might die," said Carl.

"Yes, she surely will," said Gula, agreeing with her younger brother.

While they stood discussing the situation, the old woman sat observing them. Gula noticed her eyes appeared to change colour and twinkle. She saw Gula looking at her and she smiled.

"You little one are a very wise child. They have named you after your mother," she said.

"Oh no!" exclaimed Eleanor. "My name is Eleanor, not Gula."

"I don't mean you, dear," replied the old woman. "I mean the Goddess who is up there," she said, pointing towards the sky.

Phillip laughed.

"You see what I mean? Do you get my point, Eleanor?" he asked. "She is talking about Mary, the mother of Jesus."

"I most certainly am not," replied the woman a little sternly. "There are lots of mothers and fathers up there. Also there are lots of Gods and Goddesses too, not only angels," she told them.

Phillip shook his head in sympathy at what he believed was the old woman's madness.

"Come with us mother, we'll help to find you a safe place to stay, where you'll have food, warmth and clean clothes." Phillip sounded reassuring.

"Yes," agreed Eleanor. "She can have some of my clothes too, and a coat."

"I'll give her one of my knitted hats, with a scarf and gloves to match." Gula offered with a smile.

"Perhaps a few of my socks might fit her," suggested Carl.

"She can try on my shoes and a pair of my boots too," Eleanor suggested, "Although her feet look so tiny, I do believe that Gula's shoes will fit her better than any of mine."

With the decision made, Phillip picked up the bundle of sticks and started to walk away.

"Come along mother, let's go home," he said.

"You are both kind loving people and these children are pure in heart and because of that, they shall surely revisit their home one day."

"What is she saying now?" asked Phillip.

The old lady ignored him, and so did the others because they were more interested in what the old lady had to say.

"You, little lady, daughter of the Goddess Gula, you have come down for a purpose. You were born with inherited gifts from those high ones up there," she said, pointing towards the sky. It was the Goddess who placed the name in your parents heads, the very second they opened their mouths to name you Sara Elizabeth."

Eleanor looked surprised, but Phillip did not, he gave the old woman a suspicious look.

"You are a blessed child," continued the old lady. "Powerfully gifted, a seer and healer just like your mother. She is watching over you," she added, and taking Gula's hands in hers, she kissed them. "As an angel in human flesh, you were sent to help save the world from total destruction, set from the craftiness of the evil one. Your mother has already encountered him."

On hearing that, Eleanor gasped.

"Did you hear that, Phillip? Are you listening to the prophecy?"

Phillip grumbled.

The old lady then turned to Carl.

"And you little one; noble, honest, fair and true, son of two great unions; a God and a Goddess. You volunteered to come down to go on this mission. You will remember your abilities in time, little Wobniar," she added, then looked directly at Phillip, who was trying hard to suppress his surprise.

"You are mistaken," he coughed, "Our son's name is Carl, not, well, his name is Carl," he flustered.

"The name Carl, it is not so bad. It is true," she smiled at Carl. "Indeed he will always be free."

This time there was nothing Phillip could do to conceal the look of astonishment on his face.

"Your abilities little one, they are many, and you will be as you were up there," she said, pointing again before she added, "invincible and changeable. You young boy, will be one of a group of friends, and you Gula, will join

26

them. There is much more, but I cannot tell all - that will come directly from those above in the higher realms."

The old lady's voice rose a little higher than before.

"I've wandered the earth for 500 years because of my disobedience, and now that I have seen you two with my own eyes, and have delivered the message, I will be allowed into the higher realms once more. I can return home, no more to roam the world, and I am so glad," she said.

They all saw how the woman's face lit up as she spoke and, for the first time, they perceived her in a different light. She was no longer the old woman collecting sticks by the roadside. They knew she was someone very special, even though they didn't know who she was.

She touched the cheeks of Gula and Carl, as they smiled up at her. Immediately she was transformed into a beautiful tall being. Her eyes were as green as the far depths of the ocean, her skin was the colour of bronze, and her hair was long, black and curly.

"You two will be among the most powerful seven, and one will be a feline, that much more I can say."

While the lady spoke, they also noticed that she was no longer dressed in the filthy ragged coat and shawl, but in a beautiful lilac gown. In place of the bundle of sticks, a golden sceptre appeared in her right hand, and on her head was a golden jewelled diadem. They all saw that she was majestic.

She looked at them as they stood awestruck, but as they attempted to kneel before her, she forbade them.

"It is I who should be kneeling before you, as I will when the time comes," she told them.

They also noticed that she was no longer wearing the plaited sandals; her feet were shod in shoes that sparkled like diamonds.

"She reminds me of the Angel Gabriel, mummy," said Gula.

The lady smiled again.

"I said you were as wise as you are noble, my child, I am of the same essence. My mission is complete," she said, "and now I must leave."

Phillip was dumbstruck, as he, Eleanor and the children stood and watched in adoration, when the angelic being, who had visited with them and told them a little of the past and a little of things to come, ascended into the clouds. It was as if she had become one of the stars, with others like her, waiting perhaps, at the gates of heaven.

Phillip suddenly felt silly and regretted his disbelief.

At home for the rest of the day, they thought about the amazing things they had seen and heard while continuing to celebrate Gula's birthday.

They were confused, but very excited. The children promised not to mention to anyone what had taken place and had already forgotten the woman's reference to a feline.

Over the following 12 months, one thing Gula and Carl longed for was a pet of their own. They played with their friends' pets, but it wasn't the same as having a pet of their own.

Finally, Phillip and Eleanor decided that they could have one. Their first choice – because it didn't need walking or much looking after, was a shoal of expensive tropical fish in a large tank with an electric pump. Within a few months, all the fish caught a disease and died.

Then the children were allowed to have little finches. They were supposed to be songbirds, but they refused to sing. They lived for no more than a month, caught a chill and died. Their next pet was a rabbit, which they warmed to immediately. It was as white as snow, with hazel-coloured eyes, and a squint in one eye. They called it Lucky. As no one had bothered to find out its sex, the children decided it was a girl because it was so gentle and timid. Lucky used to crawl onto their laps to sleep.

Gula and Carl cried one morning when they woke to find that Lucky was not in her hutch in the back garden. They searched and searched, but the rabbit had disappeared. In the end, they decided she must have been stolen, as she could not have escaped on her own from the hutch. Months after their sad loss, they learned from a neighbour's four-year-old son that Lucky had been taken to the children's nursery down the road by another neighbour. Not wanting to investigate the matter, Phillip and Eleanor decided to let the nursery keep Lucky.

The family bought another white rabbit, which they decided was a boy because it was so wild and frisky. Carl dubbed the crazy new rabbit Mad Max. They had begun to get fond of Max when one morning a few weeks later they awoke to find him dead in the hutch. They buried him under the apple tree they had planted at the bottom of the back garden, and in no time the tree, which had never produced any fruit, began to thrive and blossom.

One by one, they had lost all their pets. They now decided they only wanted one more pet – a cat. They pleaded for months and months, but Eleanor and Phillip kept refusing without explaining why.

They became tired of pleading and eventually gave up - until one day on the school playground...

"Carl, Craig, you'll never guess," said Tom, excitedly.

"Guess what?" asked Carl.

"Yeah, what?" asked Craig, grumpily.

"Hildegarde," replied Tom.

"What about her?" asked Craig, not really interested.

"She is pregnant. Lady H is going to have kittens!" Tom exclaimed.

There was real excitement in Tom's voice that day.

"Is she?" asked Carl, his eyes widening.

"Yeah, she is going to have kittens," repeated Tom.

Mary was skipping with her friends when she heard Craig's yells.

"Hey! Irish eyes Mary!" he shouted.

She dropped the skipping rope, much to the annoyance of her friends, and hurried over to him. She was cross, but changed her mind when Craig announced.

"Tom's cat, she's pregnant."

Mary jumped, clapping her hands.

"Oh goody goody!" she cried, smiling happily.

When Carl arrived home that afternoon after school, he told his sister the news. Gula was excited. The two children harboured a secret wish that their parents would let them have one of Hildegarde's kittens. They hadn't spoken to Tom about it yet, but they intended to, and they felt sure he wouldn't say no.

Chapter Three

A Surprise for Tom

Finally the day had come, and it was a special day in Tom's home. Hildegarde, Tom's pet cat, was about to give birth, and everyone who had gathered to see the great event was excited. Tom's family consisted of his dad Leslie, his mum Pollyanna, and his sister, Lucy. Craig, one of Tom's best friends, had also come.

Only Leslie and Pollyanna had seen a birth before. Leslie had been there when Tom and Lucy were born, so he knew about human births, which he claimed were different from animals. To be on the safe side, he had done his research on cat births and made sure everyone in the family had read up on the subject too.

What made the excitement even greater was that Mr Hixson, the local vet, had told Tom and his friends, Craig and Carl, something surprising at his last examination of Hildegarde.

"I hope your cat box will be big enough, Tom lad," he said, straightening up to reveal how tall and handsome he was.

Tom's eyes widened.

"Why, Mr Hixson? Why must Hildegarde's box be a big one?" he asked.

"Because my son, it is possible that Lady Hildegarde here, will not be giving birth to one or two kittens, but it is highly likely, as far as I can count..." Mr Hixson paused and gently felt Hildegarde's belly once more. "Don't look so apprehensive son," he continued, 'It is quite common for cats to give birth to as many as four, maybe five little ones." He smiled at Tom. Craig and Carl nudged each other and grinned. Tom looked from the vet to his friends, showing surprise. The two boys looked at each other again and giggled.

"I can have one," Craig informed them excitedly. "I am sure mother won't mind, and anyway, I have already asked her."

"You asked your mum already, how's that?" asked Carl.

"Because mum said that it is very unusual for a cat to give birth to just one kitten."

"I know that," said Carl in his usual quiet voice, "plus the vet just said so," he added. "If there are more than two, I doubt if my mum will let me have one. She doesn't like cats. I don't think so, not after..."

Carl stopped and turned towards Hildegarde, looking crestfallen.

"Not after what Carl? Go on tell us, we won't tell Jack or anyone else, I promise," Craig assured him, with all the sincerity he could muster.

Carl said no more, but gave Craig a sceptical look.

"We all know what your promises are worth," Tom said. "Besides, I don't remember telling anyone I was giving away any of my kittens," he added, pretending to be serious.

Tom gently stroked Hildegarde as he helped Mr Hixson to put her back into her carrier, and then he swallowed with a gulp.

"I suppose I had better go down to Jewels, and ask Mary to get her mum to save me the largest box from the pile in her cellar. Mary told me yesterday that her mum had them in a corner ready to give to Mr Baker in the morning, when his truck comes for the rubbish."

Mary's mother, Siobhán, and her father, Noel, had their double garage converted into a little shop two years ago, selling fancy jewellery and other interesting fair trade products. Mary loved helping in the shop most evenings after school, to earn extra pocket money. She was saving up for the new bicycle she so dearly wanted.

"Well, in that case son," said Mr Hixson, "you had better hurry because if my hunch is right, Lady H here will commence birthing tonight, certainly no later than the early hours of tomorrow morning."

"How can you tell all that, Sir?" asked Craig brightly.

"It's one of the things a vet is trained to know, apart from giving injections, seeing to fleas and all the other care that comes with the job," replied Mr Hixson, ruffling Craig's blond hair.

Craig gave the vet a disapproving look before proceeding to rearrange his hair to his liking. Carl and Tom chuckled, and Mr Hixson looked on, smiling.

The examination and questions and answers came to an end. Tom strained with the heavy carrier from the room to the surgery door, where Monica the receptionist stood holding the door open for them to leave. Craig and Carl followed behind Tom. Mr Hixson had also come out and was seated behind the desk. He had proceeded to type up Hildegarde's notes in preparation for Monica to bill Tom's parents, because he wanted the letter to catch the last post.

Tom rested the carrier on the floor by the front door before turning to face the vet.

"Mr Hixson," he called.

"Yes son," replied the vet, looking up from his work.

"Thank you Sir," said Tom, giving a faint smile.

"That's all right lad," said Mr Hixson happily.

"Mr Hixson," continued Tom after a brief pause.

"What is it laddy?" asked Mr Hixson thoughtfully.

"I hope you won't think me rude or dis-re-spect-ful Sir," remarked Tom, breaking up the long word in order to pronounce it correctly. "I do wish you wouldn't keep calling me 'son' and 'lad' or 'laddy'," he said timidly. "I really would prefer it if you called me Tom."

Tom emphasised his name as if to enforce it. Mr Hixson's face changed colour, from a pale pink to a reddish hue.

"All right Tom, as you wish, no offence taken lad. From this day on I will respect your wishes, Tom it shall be."

"Thank you Sir, Mr Hixson," Tom stammered politely, feeling a little embarrassed.

He looked from the vet to Monica, then at his two friends, who were standing outside the shop sharing the load of the carrier. They were both giggling so much that the carrier was shaking.

"Stop shaking it!" yelled Tom, rather sharply, grabbing hold of the carrier as it tipped sideways. "Suppose you drop her? Stupid," he remarked, looking disgruntled.

The three boys hurried over to Pollyanna, who was seated with Lucy in her red Peugeot estate she had parked on a yellow line.

"Be quick you lot!" snapped Pollyanna, in an agitated manner. "I had no idea it would take so long or I would not have parked here," she grumbled. "You ought to thank your lucky stars the traffic warden didn't come along. Otherwise, I would be deducting money from your pocket money every week Tom," she declared in a huff, glancing at the clock on the dashboard and at the watch on her wrist.

"Come on now," Craig interrupted, his eyebrows knitting up in disbelief. "That is so not fair," he remarked.

Craig noticed Pollyanna freeze.

"Excuse me Pollyanna, I am sorry, but you are the adult here," he continued, ignoring the stunned look on Pollyanna's face, "you chose to park where you shouldn't, so how is it Tom's fault?"

Pollyanna was still in a state of disbelief, and Craig did not give her a chance to respond.

"Lucy! Don't just sit there gawping, come and open the boot so we can put the cat in," he yelled.

The boys were finding it a strain lifting the carrier with the pregnant cat sprawled out inside it.

"Yeah," Carl agreed boldly, letting go of the carrier as the door opened.

Lucy had deliberately taken her time opening the boot of the car, causing the carrier to land with a bump as Craig abruptly released his hold. Lucy grinned mischievously.

"Watch it!" cried Tom, looking alarmed. "Be gentle with my cat, didn't you hear what Mr Hixson said? I don't want her going into labour and having her kittens in mum's car."

"Are you four getting into this car or do I drive off and leave you to it?" asked Pollyanna finding her voice, although she still looked cross.

They bundled into the car, the three boys sitting in the back seat. Lucy practically threw herself into the front seat, after glancing at the boys scornfully.

"Why are you looking at us like that skinny?" asked Tom, agitatedly.

Lucy went pale and turned to face her mother.

"Mum," she moaned.

"Right!" exclaimed Pollyanna, hitting the steering wheel in frustration as the car jerked and stalled.

"If the four of you don't stop bickering this minute..." came her stern warning, pointing her finger from one to the other, "you can all get out of my car and walk home."

"Me, I'm not walking," put in Carl, trying to raise his voice, but failing. "I wasn't bickering and I never said a word, so I shouldn't be included in this. I need a lift home, if you don't mind Pollyanna. It's three miles and my mum will be worried." He looked anxious.

"Three miles, you reckon," snapped Lucy. "Anyway, your mum, she won't be worried 'cause I'll tell her," she teased.

"You will tell her what?" Craig demanded defensively.

"Why mum chucked you lot out of the car."

Lucy blushed as she finished.

"Lucy," said Craig, fuming, "for some time I have been wondering what sort of person you really are; now I know."

"Oh yeah, what am I then?" she asked.

Craig looked as though he was about to burst with rage.

"You are a miserable, selfish little brat, that's what you are," he announced crossly.

"I am sorry Lucy, but you asked for that," said Pollyanna. "Didn't you hear me? I didn't just say the boys. I mean all four of you will be walking home, and I will speak to Eleanor, thank you."

Pollyanna stalled the car twice before she finally moved off rather bumpily.

Eight-year-old Lucy sat sulking with two fingers twisting a section of her shoulder-length light brown hair into a ringlet. As the curl soon fell out, she pulled a face that emphasized her freckles.

She began sucking her pink thumb and the noise was so annoying to the others that Pollyanna turned on the car radio. The boys removed their hands from their ears and breathed a sigh of relief.

The boys had been friends since pre-school and were 'as thick as thieves.' Tom was the eldest of the three boys. Craig was younger than Tom, by four months, but he was tall - a few more inches of growth and his head would touch the roof of Pollyanna's car.

Carl, though not the shortest, was the youngest by ten months. He was a slender, handsome 10-year-old boy who looked even younger than he was.

Carl hated wearing his Afro hair long, for fear that it would become tangled and prove troublesome to comb. On his regular visits to the barber's, he always asked for a close cut. Carl sat looking as meek as a lamb. Only his slanting eyes occasionally blinked, which emphasised his long eyelashes.

One of Tom's blue eyes was always partly hidden by his brown hair, which he would move away from his face with a quick flick of his hand. He would never agree to a haircut without an argument. The only time he would willingly have it done was for special occasions.

He was transfixed in his seat. This was a stance he adopted when forced into silence. No doubt he was daydreaming in his own private Wonderland, only not with a little dog, but with his beloved pet cat, Hildegarde. He wore his shirt sleeves rolled up, exposing the paleness of his arms, as he rested one on the edge of the car door.

Tom had kept his fair English complexion well-hidden from the summer sun.

Craig sat with his mouth open, as if waiting to get a word in. But no one was talking so he could have been trying to catch a fly that was buzzing around in the car, in his mouth!

Unlike Tom, Craig had caught the sun that summer and his tanned skin contrasted markedly with his favourite navy blue jeans and long-sleeved shirt. His clothes were clean, but in need of ironing, and his blonde hair spread out all over a rather large head, highlighting his long face.

It wasn't until Pollyanna pulled up outside Carl's gate that Craig and Tom spoke.

"Bye Carl," they said rather quietly, almost at the same time.

Lucy pulled a long face, which Carl ignored. Instead, he waved and ran straight through the open gateway to the front door of his home and pressed the doorbell forcefully.

"Mum," he called. "Quick, open the door!" he yelled through the letter-box. "I need to use the toilet, hurry up, please mum," he begged.

Tom and Craig laughed, and Lucy stuck out her tongue.

"Lucy, don't be so childish," Pollyanna scolded then she waved and blew the car horn before she sped away.

Eleanor, who had been watching Carl's hasty approach, rushed to the front door brushing her auburn hair back into place with her left hand.

"What's the matter son?" she asked anxiously.

Carl paused before his mother then began to march on the spot with his left hand between his thighs.

"Have you forgotten that you have a key for this door?" asked Eleanor.

"No mum I haven't forgotten," replied Carl, in haste.

"Who has upset you, Carl?" Eleanor asked, looking concerned.

"No one mum, honest," replied Carl, rubbing his knees together and holding on to the zipper of his trousers.

To avoid any further delays, he pushed past his mother and dashed up the stairs.

"I am okay, really mum, no one's upset me. I didn't want to wet myself."

"Is that all?" asked Eleanor, who stood looking up the stairs after him.

"Yes mum, that's all," replied Carl.

He rushed into the toilet, undoing the zipper on his brown pants at the same time. He had forgotten to close the toilet door in his rush.

"Aah! Gosh, dear me, that was a close one!"

Eleanor heard her son's voice coming from the upstairs landing. She smiled and shook her head.

"Don't forget to wash your hands," she shouted from the kitchen.

Chapter Four

How Many Kittens

Tom wasted no time that afternoon. As soon as Hildegarde was comfortable in her basket, he trotted the half a mile down to the shop.

"Mary, Mary," he called from the gate, then paused, panting to catch his breath by the front door.

Mary opened the door, her large brown eyes widening even more at the sight of Tom.

"Did you get my message? I left it on, to-"

"Stop breathing so heavily, sit down and calm yourself," interrupted Mary in a gentle manner. She pointed a stout finger at the chair in the hallway.

"Mum got it ready for you, look!" she exclaimed, and pointed again, but this time to a large cardboard box beside the telephone table.

Her eyes twinkled as she spoke, and Tom remembered how Craig regularly teased Mary because of her beautiful eyes, by singing, 'When Irish Eyes are smiling', over and over until he laughed. At that moment Tom understood why Craig reacted so childishly in Mary's presence - he was besotted with her, just as he, Tom, was. He felt like singing the same tune to Mary, to let her know how much he admired her and her eyes, but then he recalled how Carl would become offended by it and, for a second, Carl's unsmiling face flashed before him.

Tom also remembered that Mary found the teasing irritating, and at times would become cross.

"You boy who's overgrown and as fine as a beanstalk, as my father would say, I find you most infuriating right now. I just want you to know that," she would add with a nod of her head.

Tom also recalled how dignified Mary would look, just as she looked now standing before him. Mary would wave her hand to dismiss Craig from her presence, which soon snapped him out of his thoughts. He didn't want to be dismissed!

Mary was short for her ten years, but full of personality. She spoke with a slight Irish accent. Her father, Noel, had travelled from the Caribbean island of Barbados to County Cork in Ireland, where he had studied business at the university for five years. It was there he had met Siobhán, and, despite many objections from family members on both sides, because of their own prejudices, they married. Within a year, Mary was born.

49

They lived in Ireland until Mary was seven years old when her parents moved to England. On the first day at her new primary school she befriended the three boys. They had been best friends ever since.

"Oh, thank you, thank you Mary," said Tom, and within seconds the box was in his hands and he was heading for the front door.

"Tom," called Mary after him, "please let me know how many kittens she's had. I have already asked mum if I can have one."

Tom turned with a broad grin.

"By the sound of it, everyone has claimed all my kittens before they are born and I'll be left as before, with just Hildegarde."

"Oh, I didn't think that you'd want another cat, Tom," said Mary apologetically.

"Yeah, perhaps one other," replied Tom. "I am glad though," he added, looking pleased.

"Glad, glad about what?" asked Mary, relaxing.

"There are at least two good homes, so far, ready for Hildegarde's kittens, and I won't have to worry that they might be neglected in any way."

Tom's smile made him look even more attractive.

"That's nice," Mary replied cheerfully.

"I'd better hurry," said Tom, "mum and dad are waiting. Why don't you come along? We are preparing, you know, getting everything ready for the birth. I mean the deliveries. Mr Hixson said there could be up to five kittens in all."

Mary gasped.

"Five kittens. Goodness me! In that case, you will have more than one extra kitten to care for, and Lady H."

"Yes, I suppose so. I was hoping that Carl would have one, but he doesn't think that his mother will allow him to have a pet cat. His mum dislikes cats."

"Why?" asked Mary in disbelief. "How could anyone not like a little kitten? That's silly, but why?" she asked.

"I don't honestly know. He wouldn't let on, but he did say later on, that he and his sister would be working on their mother," replied Tom, sounding hopeful.

"Working on their mother?"

"Yes, to try and win her over, persuade her to change her mind and let them have one of Hildegarde's kittens. That way there will be three safe homes ready for a kitten."

"I bet you he will tell me," said Mary, sounding sure of herself.

"Okay you are on. If you get it out of Carl, I will let you choose the kitten you like best, and you Mary Stuart, will have first choice, how's that?" he asked, with a broad smile.

"That's great! Thanks Tom. Wait just a minute please," she added with growing excitement.

"I'll come with you, just for a little while, if mum will let me."

Tom looked curious.

"I won't be able to stay long," said Mary. "I have to finish my homework every night before bedtime - if not, no kitten."

"Oh," said Tom frowning.

Mary ran along the hallway and into the living room calling out.

"Mum! Mum! Where are you?"

"Here dear, in the kitchen, what is it Mary?"

Siobhán turned to face her daughter, a half-peeled potato in her left hand and the potato peeler in her right.

"Mum, can I go to Tom's for a little while, please? He said I could. I just want to help him get things ready, you know, for the birth of the kittens, and I promise I'll not stay longer than half an hour, three-quarters at the most," she assured her mother.

"You'd better not stay so long! Go on then," smiled Siobhán, whose eyes shone like Mary's.

Looking at Siobhán, it wasn't hard to tell where Mary got her good looks.

"Thanks mum, you are the best," said Mary.

In no time she was walking briskly along with Tom and holding on to one side of the box.

The fact that it was a cold Friday evening did not seem to bother the two youngsters. They were used to the British weather. Although given a choice, Mary might have preferred the hot weather. She had not stopped dreaming of a hotter climate, ever since basking in the tropics for three weeks, when she was nine years old.

Apart from Mary and Carl, no one else in their little circle of friends had ever visited a hot country.

One day, in a religious education lesson, the class was having a discussion about the different islands in the West Indies. The teacher, Mrs Townsend, knew a lot about the Caribbean Islands. She had been born and bred in St Vincent, but had visited several other islands with her father who was a government official. She had also lived in Egypt for many years in her late teens.

"All those who have ever been abroad, particularly to a hot country, please raise your hands," she said to the class.

Craig was the first to raise both hands in the air, but he also announced his impending journey to the class.

"We are going for a whole month to see my grandparents in Australia, next summer," he said. "We are going for so long because it takes almost a week to get there," he exaggerated. "We will be suffering from jet lag, which will take days, if not a whole week to get over," he said, his eyes widening. "So," he continued unembarrassed, "for us to appreciate the country and to benefit from the large amount of money it will be costing my parents, I mean costing mostly my father, we are going for a whole month, which could be longer, who knows," he ended his little speech and looked delighted.

Mary informed the class excitedly that her parents had taken her to Barbados, and were planning another trip, this time to Trinidad.

"I wish we could live there," she said dreamily. She further informed them that it was now called Trinidad and Tobago, adding, "I don't know why, so please don't ask me. My dad told me it is not far from Barbados. I believe that the two islands were once joined until the British split them up, or so I was told by my father, I mean my father told me," she added, and feeling a little foolish, turned her head away from the teacher's questioning gaze.

As for Carl, when it was his turn, he spoke quietly and modestly. "I visited Jamaica twice," he said and gave a timid little smile, "and I had a boring visit to Barbados once. My parents are now planning a holiday in Egypt, and in a way I wish that I could get out of it because, I don't think I am going to like it."

"And why is that Carl?" interrupted Mrs Townsend.

Carl's voice went even quieter.

"Oh, because I don't like what I already know about Egypt."

The teacher tried to ask another question, but Carl continued quickly. "I am sorry, but I don't want to explain what I have read that I don't like about Egypt, it's just too much to put into words."

Carl's reluctance to go to Egypt was nothing to do with anything he had read. The real secret reason was the frightening image which kept flashing through his mind. As he sat there in the classroom facing the teacher, the vision came into his mind again forcing him to hold on to the desk in front of him.

In his vision, Carl saw himself living in a palace in ancient Egypt, dressed in royal clothes. He had first seen the images in a dream, which became more and more vivid and detailed every time it returned to haunt his sleep. There were other people in the dream, but they remained vague apparitions, and he would always wake up startled and perplexed.

Forcing his mind back into the present moment, he told the class, "On the other hand, this holiday was planned to coincide with the Easter school holiday, so once I get there I might just like it, especially if mum and dad take me to the Valley of the Kings, but I will refuse to enter any of the pyramids."

Mrs Townsend smiled at Carl.

Craig and Tom, who were seated nearest to him, whispered.

"Good, Carl."

"I am glad you think so," he replied.

The children began to whisper amongst themselves, so the teacher gave them a few minutes to talk before she stood up. She was a tall impressive figure, and this movement brought instant silence. She briefly told the class about each of the countries, occasionally playing with her long curly hair as she spoke. She then told them to bring in for the next lesson a souvenir from a trip.

"I shall expect each of you to talk about the meaning of your item. It doesn't matter whether your item did not come from a Caribbean island, as long as it is from a different country. Perhaps you or your parents bought back a religious relic..." She paused. "What is a relic? A relic is something of importance, interesting because of its age and use, something from the very distant past, is the best way I can explain the meaning of the word at the moment. Do you all understand what a relic is, class?"

"Yes, Mrs Townsend," chorused nearly all the children, except for Nikhil and Naomi.

"Nikhil, and you Naomi, of all the children here, should know all about relics. Your parents' countries of origin are full of interesting and priceless relics."

Nikhil, whose parents had come over from India in the early sixties, beamed with pride, while Naomi, who had

57

been brought over to England from Japan as a baby, by her Japanese mother and English father, looked bashful.

"As an idea," continued the teacher, "you may bring in a musical instrument, and I don't mean that everyone should bring one either; we want a variety of objects to talk about. Is that clear?"

"Yes, Miss," chorused the children for the second time.

Luke, who was looked upon as a comedian by his friends, whispered to Tom.

"Another boring lesson ahead."

Unfortunately for him, his whisper wasn't soft enough.

"In that case, Luke Reid," said Mrs Townsend in her calm voice, "you will bring to the class, together with your item of interest, 30 lines, written on lined paper, explaining to everyone else why you find the lessons boring."

She smiled and Luke blushed.

"Good afternoon class, remember to go straight home now, no loitering. See you all next week, and have a good weekend."

Mary shivered a little then she looked up at Tom.

She blew warm air from her mouth, which mingled in with the white fog that was slowly forming in the air.

She looked at Tom again and they smiled at each other, instinctively tightening their grip on the cardboard box, a confirmation perhaps, of the task ahead, which was more important than worrying over a little cold weather.

The two youngsters walked briskly along, smiling and talking. Evidently contented, they appeared to embrace the cold winds that began to blow.

The wind died down as swiftly as it had come, but it left a dense fog, which seemed to be getting thicker and thicker as the two youngsters journeyed along, and it became difficult to see ahead. They were oblivious of the large, thick dark shadow that suddenly appeared some distance away. The street lights flickered and went out. Tom's left foot missed the pavement and he stumbled.

"Gosh!" Mary exclaimed. "Are you okay, Tom?"

"Yes, I'm okay," Tom replied.

The street lights flickered again and came back on, but they were much dimmer than before. Tom looked ahead and saw a large shadow surrounded by the swirling whitish-grey fog.

"What's that?" he asked.

Mary looked to where Tom was pointing.

"Where?" she asked.

"Look straight ahead, in the middle of the road. It looks as if the fog is changing colour," suggested Tom, staring.

"Oh yes," agreed Mary, in a quiet voice. "I have never seen black fog before, that's strange." She frowned.

As they continued, the solid dark shadow remained large and visible, but appeared to move further away.

"It doesn't look like fog to me," said Mary.

Tom strained his eyes to try and discern what it was. The strange shape was drifting along way ahead of them.

"No, it doesn't," he agreed. "It looks like a large elongated figure of some kind, but I can't say what it might be."

"It looks like some sort of animal to me," suggested Mary.

"What kind of animal could be so large?" asked Tom.

Mary shrugged in silence.

"There is a bus stop ahead," said Tom.

"Shall we wait for the bus?" Mary asked timidly.

"You aren't afraid are you Mary?"

"Yes, I am a little," she admitted, as the hand holding her side of the box began to shake.

"You're trembling!" said Tom.

"Yes, I am beginning to feel rather cold," said Mary, sheepishly.

Tom knew the source of her shivers was not her cold hands, but the dark shadow lingering in the fog.

"We can wait for the bus if you like," he suggested, "but we've nearly reached the bridge. Look, there it is."

Tom pointed to their left. Mary looked and saw the bridge looming up across the sombre waters of the River Thames. They instinctively looked ahead again at the middle of the road. The dark shadow had almost disappeared, but it had left behind a menacing sound, which reverberated through their heads.

"No animal I know makes that kind of sound," said Tom.

"I agree," said Mary, anxiously.

In the distance the fog was still dense, but whitish-grey again.

Both Tom and Craig lived on a man-made island, just off the busy high street of a Middlesex town. To reach the small island they had to walk across one of the bridges across the River Thames.

The island's main business had been boat building, until publishing, art and crafts and a few other companies became established.

The homes were mainly weather-boarded shacks, terraced cottages and bungalows. Some houses close to the banks would flood when it rained heavily, despite the high protective walls. A few people lived in boathouses on and off the river, and barges regularly sailed up and down its waters.

The quaint little place was dimly lit at night, and many overhanging tree branches heightened the mysterious atmosphere.

As Tom and Mary were crossing the bridge, Tom noticed that Mary's hand was no longer shaking. He smiled at her and she smiled back. He took a large torch from his rucksack, switched it on, and the large circle of light brightened the path leading to his home.

Tom and Mary walked along the torch-lit path and through the garden gateway to his home. The house was surrounded by lots of black and white cats, all snarling, growling and howling.

Mary was frightened and ran to the door. She did not wait for Tom to open it. Instead, she kept her finger on the doorbell until Leslie opened it.

"What's all this in aid of? Isn't one ring enough?" he asked, frowning.

"Sorry dad," said Tom.

"Yes, I am sorry Mr Harper, but-"

Tom interrupted grinning.

"Mary got scared dad because there are about 12 cats surrounding the house."

"Oh, they must be here because of the impending birth of one of their own kind. That's nice," suggested Leslie.

"I don't think so dad. They sounded pretty awful," admitted Tom.

"Creepy and scary is more like it," said Mary.

"Never mind about the cats outside," said Leslie. "They didn't hurt you did they, Mary?"

"No, I guess not," she replied.

Leslie looked down at the cardboard box in Tom's hand.

"You've got the box. That's good. Let's go and prepare Hildegarde's bed," he encouraged.

Craig was allowed to stay over, at least until Hildegarde gave birth, although his mother, Stella, had hinted that since Monday would be a bank holiday, which meant no school, she wouldn't mind if he stayed a day or two.

Stella was always dumping Craig on other people so she could go dancing with his father. His parents loved ballroom dancing, and the tango was their favourite. Craig didn't seem to mind. He enjoyed being with his best friends, unless it was a family gathering and his favourite grandmother, Evelyn - who always brought him a present - was coming, then he would be happy to stay at home.

Craig had already chosen a name for his kitten, and everyone had laughed when he announced it rather loudly, in a posh accent.

"I am going to call my kitten Cleo if it is a girl but, if it is a boy, I shall call him Tigger."

Mary refused to let on what name, if any, she had chosen for her kitten.

"That would be telling, and wouldn't you like to know," was her reply when asked.

Carl, who hoped his mother would let him have a kitten, made his announcement timidly.

"I would call my cat Clovis, if it's a 'him', but I don't know yet what I would call it, if it's a 'she'."

"I like that name Carl," said Craig, in a pleasant tone of voice.

"Yes," chorused Tom and Mary.

Lucy smirked.

Carl looked at Lucy and gave a confident little smile, as though to say, 'Those who really matter to me didn't smirk; they liked the name I have chosen and have said so. So you can smirk all you like, it doesn't bother me'.

"If Carl is not allowed to have a kitten, and I choose a male, I would like to call him Clovis, to honour Carl, of course," Mary announced, to everyone's surprise.

"Of course," Craig mimicked mischievously.

Mary had a crush on Carl, but Carl was too shy and innocent in his ways to encourage her.

Like Mary, Carl wasn't permitted to sleep over, but he had been allowed to stay until 10pm that night. Phillip would pick him up in the car.

Craig and Tom had promised to keep Carl informed about further developments.

Early that Friday evening, Tom and his friends, Craig, Carl, Mary and even Lucy, helped Pollyanna and Leslie with the weekend cleaning. They all made sure that Hildegarde was as comfortable as possible, and that everything was ready and in place for the multiple birth of the baby kittens.

It was an excited household, but the excitement was mingled with Tom's concern for the mother cat, as Hildegarde was either lying down exhausted, or hobbling around slowly, looking grossly overweight.

They all followed Leslie's instructions, and in no time they heard the alarm on Mary's watch go off. She had set it to make sure she kept the promise to her mother to leave for home on time. She was determined nothing would hinder her from getting the kitten of her dreams. She had also vowed that she would be the nicest, most obedient daughter anyone ever had. Immediately the alarm went off, Mary stopped it and waved goodbye to the others. As soon as she stepped out of the house, she rang her mother.

"Mum," she said, "it is exactly 5.30pm and I am on my way home."

"Good girl," said Siobhán. "See you soon, darling. Dinner is ready and daddy is home. We won't start without you, sweetheart."

"Thanks, mum, here comes the bus, I'll see you in 10 to 15 minutes. I love you, mum."

Mary cut off the phone and jumped on the bus before her mother had a chance to respond.

Leslie and Pollyanna knew that pregnant cats were quite capable of taking care of themselves. They had read a lot about labour and birthing, checking and rechecking every detail to make sure everything went as smoothly as possible for Hildegarde.

They had already kept her away from other pets and strangers, especially children, due to the fact that female cats can become aggressive in the last stages of pregnancy, but all those gathered nearby were no strangers to Hildegarde. She had jumped on their laps many a time before becoming pregnant. They were the same humans with whom she played ball and string games. They had also taken turns to take her food and fresh water, and to make sure her basket was always dry and clean. They had cuddled and groomed her, and had fretted whenever she wandered off with a friend, and would go searching for her, calling her name until they found her.

"Lady H, Lady H, where are you?"

They loved her and she knew it.

On this special occasion, Tom was worried whenever Hildegarde attempted to walk.

"Please, dad, help me to keep her calm. She is not supposed to become so active, and don't you think we should put her in her bed, mum?" he asked.

Everyone looked at Tom with sympathy. They understood his concern because, to him, Lady H was no ordinary cat. She was a blue blood, a pedigree; her mother was taken from the royal household of cats in Egypt. Tom did not voice it, but somewhere deep inside him, he feared that he might lose his special and precious pet.

They had created a maternity bed out of the large cardboard box that Tom fetched from Mary's mother, after Leslie had checked to make sure the box had a lid, because it would help to keep the newborn kittens warm and safe. Leslie also cut a hole in one side of the box, large enough so that Hildegarde would be able to crawl in and out.

Lucy was allowed to place the shredded newspaper in the bottom of the box, which Carl covered after he folded a rather large blanket in two; Craig's mother made it from three of his old shirts.

Finally, Pollyanna and Leslie lifted the box and placed it not too far from the radiator in the living room, even though the room was quite warm. They also had a lovely log and coal fire blazing. They made sure that the box was away from any draught that might escape into the room, as they were going in and out quite frequently, before they finally settled down.

Earlier, Leslie had explained to the group that without all the preparations, Hildegarde might find a place of her own to deliver her kittens, which could even be in the bottom of a wardrobe or another of her favourite spots.

There was every possibility that Hildegarde might still choose to do just that, since they had only just got her box bed ready.

No sooner were the preparations finished, when the doorbell of the Harper's house rang. It was Carl's dad.

"See you later Tom," said Carl.

After thanking his friend's parents, Carl left with his father. That whole weekend, Carl's sister Gula, prayed a lot, and surprisingly, even Carl, who had never liked to say prayers, joined in.

There were several Holy Mary, mother of God prayers and even angels of God prayers, which ended with, 'In the name of the Father, Son and Holy Spirit', and 'Dear God, please take away the fear of cats from mummy and let her say yes to us having one of Tom's kittens'! Carl never forgot to add, looking up at the ceiling, a big, 'Thank you, wherever you lot are up there. I do hope you can all hear me, and I will never pray to you again, if mum and dad, don't let us have one of Lady H's kittens, amen'.

The prayers could be heard both mornings and evenings coming from two of the bedrooms in the McKenzie household. They were said so loudly, that Eleanor and Phillip could hear every word except for the last part of Gula's prayer. Those were the bits she whispered to an Egyptian Goddess Bastet, and they made Carl frown.

The kittens were not yet born, but Carl's anxiety was growing. He feared that his prayers would not be answered and he would not get the pet cat he longed for.

On this rather nice sunny day, Eleanor had organised a garden party for Carl and his friends. Whilst enjoying a treasure hunt, which Gula arranged, Carl saw something glowing at the bottom of the garden, behind a tree. He rushed towards it, believing that he had found the largest and most important hidden present wrapped in gold, but as he got closer, he saw how large it was. He stopped suddenly, seeing that it was not a large wrapped parcel, but instead a glowing bush.

"Wow," he whispered, "the bush is on fire!"

Carl, not believing what he saw, reached out towards it, but quickly pulled his hand back.

The bush blazed, but with no heat. In the middle of it sat a tabby cat, looking up at him. Around the cat's head, was a golden diadem adorned with priceless gems of different colours.

Carl tried to turn away, but could not, so he opened his mouth to call the others, but his tongue felt heavy and he could not speak.

"Step inside the bush, Carl," said a voice from the bush. Carl's tongue suddenly became loose.

"I don't know who you are, but you must be crazy," he replied. "Is this your cat?"

"No, the feline does not belong to me, but to a higher order. Boy, step inside the bush," the voice commanded.

"No, I will not step inside that fire. I don't want to die," said Carl.

He tried to step backwards, away from the fiery bush, but his legs felt too heavy to move.

"You must overcome your fear Carl, and step inside this bush. Or one day your fear may become your weakness, and a mission set for you, will fail, unless you conquer it now. Yes, this bush burns, but there is no fire. Reach out Carl, reach out now and touch it."

Carl obeyed. He reached out slowly and pushed his hand into the bush, smiling because it did not burn him. He felt no pain and when he looked at his hand, it was golden. He walked into the bush. He could not believe what transpired then. His whole body became golden, even the clothes he wore that day changed colour.

"You will not understand now what you have seen and heard, but in time, it will all become clear to you. Carl, a day will come when you will be forced to remember important things from the past, about who you were and what you were called. You will need to remember these things for a good reason. The creature standing beside you is about to be born to the cat, Lady Hildegarde. His nobility, among other things, will be revealed in good time."

Carl turned and looked around, but he could not see the garden with his sister and friends. He opened his mouth to speak once more.

"Carl," came the voice before him, "you will name the kitten, Clovis. Keep up the prayers and your mother, Eleanor, will overcome her fear of cats. You and your sister will have the pet you desire, but he is to be *your* pet, Carl.

"Remember also that in the future there will be times when you will need my assistance. No matter where you are, find a place where there is greenery outside. Call out the name Bastet, and the burning bush will appear. Remember that the bush will only answer to *your* voice and no other."

Carl then closed his eyes and rubbed them with both hands. When he opened them again, the golden cat had disappeared, the bush had ceased glowing and he and his clothes were no longer golden, but in his hand was an unusually large golden egg. He quickly walked away towards his friends, but turned to look behind him before he ran shouting and holding up the golden egg.

"I have it!" he exclaimed. "I have won the best prize," he said, smiling.

"Where did you get that gigantic egg, Carl," asked Nikhil. "It's amazing," he added, looking at Gula.

"I found it down the back, by that clump of green bushes," replied Carl, pointing to the bush behind the large tree in his back garden.

"I didn't put *that* there, perhaps mum did. Go and ask her," said Gula, staring at the large golden egg in surprise. Carl was holding it in his hands, as if he cherished it.

"It's mine. I found it so I'm keeping it," said Carl rather defensively, walking away.

Carl said nothing about the encounter, but it was a day he would never forget.

With the prayers came offers to accompany their parents to Mass on Sundays. There was no grumbling either when the children were asked to run an errand or to do a little housework, such as dusting or washing the dishes. In fact, many of the chores were done before they were even asked! They would take turns to wash, dry and tidy away the dishes. They would sweep and mop the kitchen floor, and even make cups of tea for mummy and daddy McKenzie. All the arguments over whose turn it was to do this or that stopped.

That Friday evening, Hildegarde lay in her maternity bed, but as the night drew on, she became restless and began to pace around the room, like someone desperately looking for a lost object.

The concerned group knew she was ready to give birth, so no one bothered to go to bed that night, and it wasn't too long afterwards that Hildegarde became vocal and began regular trips to her litter box. Those visits continued for nearly an hour before she finally settled down in her maternity bed.

"Isn't Hildegarde good?" said Leslie softly. "I really thought she would have a problem with the box, and choose one of her usual corners to have her kittens."

"She is a special cat," agreed Pollyanna.

The children looked at each other and smiled. Tom had a proud look. Hildegarde closed her eyes as if asleep, but within a few minutes her unusual behaviour told everyone the kittens were on the way.

A bowl of warm water was put in place together with clean towels, cloths, dental floss, and petroleum jelly, just in case it was needed. It wasn't long before poor Lady H's whimpers became cat screams, as she began to push out the first kitten.

Tom could hardly bear to witness his beloved pet in such discomfort and, although he had been forewarned, tears welled up in his eyes. But he didn't leave the room. Lucy was less stoic. She ran out of the room, up the stairs and into her bedroom. She pulled open her drawer, picked up her Walkman, pushed the earphones into her ears and curled up on her bed after covering herself with the duvet from head to toe.

Downstairs, Hildegarde was giving birth to her first kitten, a male, who came out head first. After the first birth, she stopped screaming, and one after another, over five hours, she gave birth calmly to four more kittens.

It was a sight to behold, and witnessed at a distance by Tom, his parents and Craig.

Everyone was delighted to see the five kittens. After each birth, Hildegarde fussed around her baby, licking it clean and doing everything a mother should, to form a strong bond. Leslie and Pollyanna were glad she was so attentive to her litter. It meant they didn't need to lend a hand to make sure the kittens could breathe.

It was in the early hours on Saturday, November 26th. Pollyanna and Leslie went into the kitchen to make some tea, leaving Lady H to tend to her babies and get some well-earned rest.

The boys remained at a distance, in a state of awe. But Leslie eventually called them into the dining room for tea and toast. Lucy, who by this time was asleep in her room, did not know the kittens were born.

They spent half an hour eating, drinking and discussing the past five hours' events. Then Tom's parents said they were tired and would go for a shower and a lie down. They also suggested the boys should get some rest too. But Tom tiptoed back into the living room quietly. He didn't want to disturb Hildegarde, but he also wanted a last peek.

Hildegarde shifted in her box as if trying to find a more comfortable spot. Tom's anxiety mounted when he realised that his cat began to push again. He hurried back into the dining room.

"Mum, dad, come back, hurry, I think another one is coming!"

"Another one? Good heavens!" remarked Leslie.

They tiptoed back into the living room and sure enough there was brave Hildegarde, giving birth to a sixth kitten, a male.

He was tiny and feeble-looking compared with his three brothers and two sisters. He looked so poorly that Leslie glanced at his son and shook his head. He was afraid to voice his fears, not wanting to alarm Tom.

Hildegarde looked at the kitten, a mirror image of herself, but she wasn't showing quite the same solicitous treatment for the sixth kitten as for the first five, which was a worry and a mystery to all the onlookers. Instead, she curled up quietly with the kitten still attached to her. Leslie and Pollyanna now stepped in to do what Hildegarde had neglected to do for her last baby kitten.

Hildegarde had failed to break the sack to enable the kitten to breathe. As quick as a flash, Pollyanna picked up a clean towel, tore the sack and gently cleaned the kitten's mouth and nose. This last arrival was a surprise for everyone, but especially for Tom.

Chapter Five

The Sixth Kitten

"Mum, dad!" exclaimed Tom. "What has happened? What is wrong with Hildegarde?"

"Sshh!" whispered Pollyanna with a finger to her lips.

"Dad," whispered Tom, "why won't she help her last kitten?"

Tom looked helpless.

"Please, Tom, try not to worry. Lady H will be okay, she is just resting, she has done a great job already," said Leslie in a low tone of voice, trying to console his son.

"Just sit quietly and let dad and me help out here, we'll do all we can for this little one," said Pollyanna, to reassure him further.

Leslie took over and gently began to dry the kitten by rubbing against the grain of his hair with a clean cloth. Pollyanna rubbed him firmly with a clean warm cloth, to dry and stimulate him, so he could take his first breath.

He then tied dental floss around the umbilical cord about an inch from the kitten's body, and then cut it. Care was taken not to cut the cord too close to the kitten, which could cause infection, even death.

Craig tiptoed over to Tom and placed a hand on his shoulder.

"Don't worry Tom. If the worst comes to the worst, and I don't feel that it will, look on the bright side my friend, you will still have five kittens, and they are all lovely." Craig continued solemnly, "Let's not be too greedy. Let's just be thankful that five kittens are fine."

"Are you saying that Lady H is not fine and neither is her last kitten?"

Tom looked pitiful, and tears welled up in his eyes.

"No," whispered Craig, "she is tired and resting. She is all right."

Tom sat with his head buried in his hands between his knees, and Craig sat down beside him watching Leslie and Pollyanna working quickly together. Tom couldn't watch anymore, but he wouldn't leave the room either. He was determined to wait to hear his parents tell him that Hildegarde's last baby kitten was out of danger. Perhaps then his heart would stop pumping so hard, it felt like it might explode inside his chest.

Craig gave a gentle cough, which attracted Leslie and Pollyanna's attention. Pollyanna paused briefly and turned to look over at him.

"Is there anything I can do to help?" Craig whispered.

Leslie and Pollyanna smiled and shook their heads, then they looked at each other, they did not speak, their eyes said it all.

Tom and Craig resolved to stay still now and not interfere with what Leslie and Pollyanna were doing, but they were both praying inside. In the agonising minutes that followed for Tom, he couldn't help but admire the dedication of his parents.

A few minutes later Leslie said the kitten was breathing, but only barely.

There were hopeful faces and sighs of relief. Craig put his hands together. He wanted to clap, but he didn't because he knew it would not only be a foolish thing to do, but might disturb Hildegarde and her babies. He pulled a long face as Leslie placed the last little one close to his mother's nipple.

Hildegarde half-opened her eyes and mouth as if to say, 'thank you', and the sad, but hopeful four, stood watching for a little while.

They all looked tired as they walked slowly, one by one, out of the room, leaving the door ajar.

Both Leslie and Pollyanna knew they had done all they could and it was time to call Mr Hixson. Tom and Craig gave Leslie and Pollyanna a huge hug. Tom felt no words could express the admiration he had for his parents at that moment. He was silent, but his face said it all.

"Let us hope for the best and pray for this last little one that miracles can happen," said Pollyanna.

"And *will* happen," put in a determined Tom.

"I will just go into my office and give Mr Hixson a call all the same," said Leslie. "I will just let him know what has happened. He may decide that under the circumstances he ought to come and check Hildegarde and her babies. I am sure he will," he added, walking towards his office.

Tom and Craig followed behind him looking dejected.

In the office Leslie picked up the receiver, but before he dialled the number, he looked at the clock on the wall.

"Oh good," he said, "it's not too early to call, I will catch him before he leaves for work."

Unlike nearly all the other children in his class at St Catherine's Primary School, religious education lessons were never boring for Tom. He could not understand the other children's moaning. He looked forward to school on

Tuesdays because that was the day he could take part in Mrs Townsend's discussions.

What made Mrs Townsend's lessons doubly interesting for him, was the fact that she taught more than religious education. Her lessons covered different cultures and involved the whole class in complicated discussions. She taught citizenship, debating the duties and responsibilities that came with being a member of a community.

Tom also loved the lessons because she didn't just talk *at* the children. She talked *with* them and shared her knowledge in such a way that everyone could grasp something positive and good out of what she was saying.

She also showed the value of whatever was said. To Mrs Townsend, everyone had a voice and everyone should be heard, so there were always class discussions in which everyone participated.

"Whatever anyone has to say in my class must be valued and listened to," she said.

At times, even when the children started to talk amongst themselves, she didn't just stop them and take over. She gave them a time to discuss, and would often sit and listen.

On one occasion Craig, in his usual bold manner, told the children to belt up. He was told by the teacher to be quiet and listen, if he could.

"Why Mrs Townsend, why did you ask Craig to be quiet and listen to a bunch of kids wasting valuable lesson time?" Kara asked.

"One never knows what thing of vital importance is being said at times like these," she replied. "Do you not think, Kara, I also know when it is time to take over? Nothing is ever as nonsensical as we believe it to be."

She gave one of her beautiful smiles, which made everyone feel happy inside.

Mrs Townsend's lessons also allowed Tom to practise speaking in front of an audience, which he said was important for his future. Tom did not intend to follow in the footsteps of his father and become an architect, or his mother, a psychotherapist, but to find his own calling. He felt passionately that he wanted to be on the stage as an actor, so what was often voiced by his peers as boring or rubbish, he found interesting and informative.

Tom was friendly with everyone. He loved people, regardless of their colour, social status or cultural background, and he carried inside him a great love for animals too, especially cats.

When he awoke on this particular Tuesday morning, he was looking forward to the discussions in Mrs Townsend's lessons even more than usual. He knew he would get the chance to talk about his long weekend, his beloved Hildegarde and the birth of her kittens. He intended starting right at the beginning. The fact that he had awoken in the early hours, his cheeks flushed from a high temperature and his head aching, didn't matter. He was so excited that he pushed the illness to the back of his mind.

He went into the bathroom, splashed cold water over his face and patted his cheeks several times with a cold flannel. He went back into his bedroom, dressed and went downstairs, where he greeted his parents as though he was feeling fine.

"Morning mum," he said, and pouted a kiss.

He did not want to touch her face for fear she would feel how hot he was and march him back up to bed. No, he had to avoid that! He didn't usually kiss his dad anymore. A hug and a handshake was good enough now that he was 12 years old, so he gave his father a quick hug and sat down to breakfast. He had two glasses of freshly squeezed orange juice and a dish of mixed fruit. The mango and pineapple bits were his favourite, so he took a second helping and was excused from eating his cereal.

Tom went off to school feeling ill, but he was also bubbling up inside as he rode off on his bike. In a little while he met up with Mary, who rode alongside him and a short while after that they were joined by Carl and Craig. Then Nikhil tagged along on his bike, although he lived closest to the school and didn't need to ride.

Throughout that morning, Tom regularly monitored the time and was caught doing so in the English lesson by Mr Edgewood.

"Tom Harper, this is the eighth time that I have seen you looking at either your watch or the clock on that wall," he said in his deep Scottish accent, pointing backwards at the clock.

Mr Edgewood had an unusually long nose, which became a regular target for jokes during the English lessons, as it seemed to grow even longer as he spoke. The children agreed that he looked like Pinocchio.

"There are ten minutes left before this class is due to end," he informed them, before sipping his water.

The children also couldn't help noticing that his cheeks were as pink as a rose, and that his face was round. In fact, his whole body was round. There were some cheeky comments about his appearance and the children giggled. Mr Edgewood slammed the white plastic mug on the table before him and spoke sharply.

"Not only will Tom get a detention and a letter to excuse him from his next lesson if he continues to watch the time in the remainder of this lesson, but the rest of you will join him!" he said. "So keep up the giggling, if that is what you are all hankering after."

There was silence as Mr Edgewood paused to clean up the water he spilled.

"Now," he said more quietly, then grinned, "That's better; perhaps we can get on with it. Where was I?" he asked.

No one answered; no one except Patricia Moline.

"Birdbrain Beaky," she whispered, which was another name they had pinned on their English teacher.

"What was that I heard?" he asked angrily.

They all sat silent and still. No one in Mr Edgewood's lesson wanted a detention because, as boring as they found Mrs Townsend's lessons, they much preferred to be in her class. The interruption took care of the rest of the lesson because the teacher glanced up at the clock.

"Is that the time already," he said. "That clock must be fast. Has anyone... say, Tom Harper, you have been keeping an eye on the time all afternoon, what time is it by your watch?"

Not giving Tom a chance to answer, Sean Scully replied.

"At the first stroke it will be, 2.33 and ten seconds."

Sean was lying. The whole class began to laugh, and poor Tom, believing that the teacher was about to hold to his threat and keep everyone behind went pale, until he heard the teacher's voice bellowing.

"Class dismissed, get out quickly, all of you."

The children scrambled out of the classroom so fast there were a few banged heads. Within minutes they were walking into Mrs Townsend's classroom on time for a change, thanks to the 'courageous fool, Sean Scully', as Luke Reid later dubbed him.

Room R6 was open, but empty, as the teacher had not yet arrived. Tom looked at his watch. It said 2.23pm, so there were seven minutes before the class was due to begin. He walked over to his desk and put down the envelope containing the pictures he wanted to show the class. Craig took the seat next to him, looked at the envelope and grinned, then he glanced at Tom.

"What animal have you chosen to talk about, Tom?" he asked. The rest of the class didn't hear Craig's question because they were busy chatting. "As if I didn't know," he continued quickly before Tom had a chance to reply.

"Yes, you know, so why ask?" said Tom.

"Because, in that case," said Craig, "we have a common interest. I too will be talking about the events over this past weekend."

"You'd better not, Craig," put in Carl, in a calm but serious manner. "That is cheating. Lady H is not your pet," he reminded Craig. "Tom," he continued, "if he does such a thing to you, I wouldn't let him have one."

"You wouldn't, would you Carl? I wonder why?" retorted Craig, sarcastically. "It wouldn't by any chance be because your mum won't let you because she doesn't like them," he mocked.

Carl was quick to respond, but he was annoyed.

"My sister and I…" he said, but as if he thought better of it, he stopped.

Tom and Mary gave Carl a friendly smile.

"Why, that's great news," Mary said encouragingly.

"You can stop pretending you are pleased, Irish eyes," interrupted Craig. "He didn't say he could have one, and anyway, wasn't it you who wanted to steal the name Carl chose?"

Craig was being spiteful.

"That was only if he wasn't allowed. Why, *you!*" Mary stamped her foot angrily. "For your information," she continued after a quick thought, "I have chosen another name for you." She pointed angrily at Craig, "Mop head!" she cried, and giving Craig a scornful look, she walked back to her seat.

"Tom," said Carl, "I hope Mrs Townsend calls you first. Let him find something else to talk about. It is so bad of him. I can't believe he would steal your talk." Carl looked at Craig and shook his head in disgust. He was disappointed and it showed.

Nikhil, who had been listening the whole time without saying a word, turned to Craig.

"He won't do that, not if he wants to continue having us as his friends," he warned.

Those nearby nodded their heads in agreement, even though they had no idea what had caused the argument. They were about to find out as the teacher walked in.

"Right, class," said Mrs Townsend. "I hope you have all done your homework, so, without wasting time..."

She sat in her seat behind the desk.

"Let us begin. We have a lot to get through in just one lesson, but..." She paused. "I will have silence class." She looked around the room. "If we run out of time and some of you don't get a chance to be heard, we will carry the same talk over to the next lesson. All in favour please let me see a show of hands."

The teacher smiled as all hands went up contentedly. Their secret was exposed; they liked the lessons after all.

"My, I do like this class," admitted Mrs Townsend unreservedly. "Now, who will be brave enough to go first?"

With no time to waste, Craig was on his feet with his hand in the air.

"Me, I will Miss, I would like to go first," he said loudly.

"No Craig, I don't think so, not this time, you are always going first. Give someone else a chance. I shall choose... Tom." The teacher looked over at Tom. "I would like Tom to begin this lesson. Do you agree class?" she asked.

Nearly the whole class stuck their hands up in the air, their heads nodding; except for one boy who sat sulking.

It was agreed that each child would stand in front of the class to give their talk.

Tom looked at the envelope on the desk before him, gave a faint smile and walked bravely up to face the audience of familiar faces. He coughed.

"I would... I would like to tell you a little about my pet cat. Her name is Hildegarde, but we call her Lady H, so if you hear me say Lady H, for short, and not Hildegarde, you will know she is one and the same pet."

Tom paused, cleared his throat again, glanced around the classroom and began to tell his story. He began with Hildegarde's origins. When it came to the bit about the sixth kitten, Carl, who dearly wanted a kitten, and even Nikhil, who wouldn't be allowed to have one and didn't want one anyway, shook their heads sadly. Mary took a tissue from her bag and blew her nose as tears stung her eyes.

"Please don't be sad," said Tom. "The vet, Mr Hixson, will be coming to check on the kittens and Lady H this evening. My parents told us to pray for a miracle, so all those of you who believe in God, perhaps you can join me. When you get home, please pray for Hildegarde. Pray that my pet's sixth kitten will live."

Tom put on a brave face and walked back to his desk. He then picked up the envelope and all eyes followed him, including Mrs Townsend's.

"I have brought some pictures of Hildegarde and her kittens with me to show you all," he informed the class. "The baby kittens are now nearly four days old."

"Yes please," cried many in the class.

"Oh good!" exclaimed the twins, Kara and Sara Buckling.

Tom looked over at Craig, who sat quietly, looking even more miserable. He gazed at Carl, who sat with a broad smile on his face.

"Please," he continued, "if you take a quick look then pass them from row to row so everyone can see them. And please, let me have all my pictures back, thank you."

Tom gave a small bow, walked back to his seat and sat down as the whole class applauded.

"All right class," said the teacher. "Please give those pictures back to Tom as quickly as possible and let us get on. We have other children to hear from before the end of this lesson." She paused, looked around and then continued. "Now Craig, let us have Craig up front, he can go next," she said.

"Actually, Miss, can I be allowed to do mine on Friday?"

"Why Craig?" asked Mrs Townsend, looking surprised. "I thought you wanted to go first. Now you are asking to present your talk on Friday." The teacher thought for a moment before she agreed. "All right Craig, you may give your talk on Friday."

"Thank you, Miss," said Craig, breathing a sigh of relief as the teacher turned to the rest of the class.

"All those who would like to give their talk on Friday, let me see a show of hands."

Over half the children held their hands up, so Mrs Townsend wrote their names down then placed the paper into her folder.

"Next, who wants to go next? Is someone going to volunteer or shall I choose? Quickly now, we haven't got all day."

Mrs Townsend waited a few seconds. "All right, I would like Deb-" but before the teacher could finish the name, Nikhil edged his way up to the front of the class.

"I don't have a pet," he announced.

"Then what are you doing up front?" asked Sally.

"Sally Standish, please be quiet and let Nikhil speak," said Mrs Townsend, in a firm voice.

Nikhil continued.

"If I was ever allowed to have a pet, I would choose a monkey." Nikhil's information caused loud laughter.

"Silence!" cried Mrs Townsend with a serious expression. Nikhil, looking embarrassed, gave a few reasons why he liked monkeys, including the fact that they ate a lot of bananas, which was his favourite fruit. This brought about more laughter.

"Monkey boy," whispered Stanley Baker, giggling.

Nikhil, blushing, cut his talk short and edged back to his seat.

Eleven children spoke about their special animals that day, and there was quite a variety, from Tom's cat and her kittens, Nikhil's wish for a pet monkey, to a hamster and a budgerigar. Someone even said they had an iguana, which surprised Mrs Townsend.

"Trevor Cartwright, have you really got a pet iguana?" she asked.

"Yes Miss, but not a large one, just a baby."

"I see," she replied, looking doubtful.

One child spoke about his talking parrot named Charlie and smiling, told the class he had taught it to say the name Camellia. Mrs Townsend smiled, and some of the children laughed. Someone else told the class about his pet guinea pig; another child spoke about a fish which had died after two days, and finally they heard about a rabbit that looked pink from a distance.

"Thanks very much to those boys and girls who have contributed to this lesson," said Mrs Townsend. She got up and walked to the front of the class.

"Not only was it an enjoyable talk, but it was also interesting and informative. Does the rest of the class agree?" she asked.

"Yes Miss," chorused most of the children.

Craig, Luke and a few others did not respond, but sat looking bored.

"Those who have bravely come up and shared with us the amazing tales about their pets deserve a hand clap. Wouldn't you say so, class?"

"Yes, Miss," they chorused again.

"Well, in that case, let's hear it for the brave presenters."

They all began to clap their hands, and even Craig, who had been sulking for some time, joined in.

"We have a few minutes left before the bell goes, so I would like to add my congratulations to you all, and I look forward to the rest of you giving your talk next lesson, so please, those of you who haven't yet presented, come prepared," said their teacher, "as it will be your last chance - I am not knowledgeable about a lot of the pets mentioned here this afternoon, but Tom's cat, Hildegarde, or Lady H, for short..."

Mrs Townsend looked over at Tom and gave a quaint smile.

"I too am a lover of cats. Cats are very intelligent animals and they are members of the feline family," she informed the class. "I am sure many, if not all of you, already know that. Cats to me are very noble animals. Whenever I see a cat, I am instinctively drawn back to

98

Egypt, and I remember Bastet, and the story that in ancient times she was the Goddess of cats, a woman with a human body, but the head of a cat. I believe that she is still worshipped today, especially at a festival called the Feast of Bastet.

"Bastet is said to be a protector and the Goddess of pleasure, dancing, music and joy. She is considered a sacred cat, and her name means 'devouring lady'. There are those who actually believe that she possessed the all-seeing eye of Ra, the sun God and a lion king. Some people believe that Bastet protects women, children and domestic cats, and is also known as the Goddess of sunrise. Cats held a high and honoured position in many households in ancient Egypt, and were looked upon as more important than human beings."

A few gasps came from around the class room.

"They were revered and looked upon as demigods in ancient Egypt, which means they were treated like Gods, but with lesser status.

"Anyone caught harming a cat, even by accident, would be killed instantly without a trial because cats guarded the royal granaries - the grain warehouses; they kept those buildings free from the vermin that threatened the food supplies."

Mrs Townsend walked over to a wooden cupboard and took out a stone image, which she placed on her desk.

"This, boys and girls, is a statue of the Goddess Bastet."

She then stood to the side of the table and glanced from the image to the children.

"That's enough about cats," she said after a while, and at that moment it was as if the teacher's hazel eyes had become larger than usual and intensely bright, like large green marbles. "Now," she said, "I want to mention Nikhil's wish, which many of you thought was hilarious. I am sure that was because none of you - apart from Nikhil - has heard that monkeys are also special animals."

The children stopped smiling and sat to attention.

"Many years ago, I was told by a Hindu scholar that the monkey is considered a holy animal in the Balinese Hindu tradition. In the *Ramayana* epic, an army of monkeys helped Rama to save queen Sita from evil. Incidentally, Sita, in Hinduism, is said to be an incarnation of the Goddess Lakshmi. In Hinduism, which is noted the main religion of India and Nepal, Rama is believed to be an incarnation of the Hindu God Vishnu. Some people may prefer to use the term avatar or personification. The Hindus are people from Hindustan; as Nikhil and his family are most probably known in their own community. They believe in the worship of God in many different forms. And so, they have many Gods and Goddesses."

The teacher gave Nikhil a pleasant smile, and he looked pleased.

"I will not say any more about this because we have very little time left today," she said.

"Lastly," she continued, "the little that I know about the iguana lizard, is that they are all green, plant-eating reptiles, and chiefly native to South and Central America. Saying that, I believe iguanas can also be found in the United States of America and some of the Caribbean islands. I have personally seen iguanas in Jamaica and St Lucia. And I am sure they can also be found in many, if not all of the African countries too." The teacher paused to glance around the room before she began again.

"I have heard that some iguanas actually grow as long as six feet, and can weigh up to twenty pounds, if not more, and about half their length is their strong whip-like tail. They are undoubtedly excellent swimmers."

Mrs Townsend paused briefly and coughed. A few children turned in Trevor's direction as the teacher continued.

"I have heard that the female iguanas can lay up to 17 eggs at any one time, and that the eggs can take up to fourteen weeks to hatch out. Apart from the leaves, they also feed on shoots and fruit."

Omotayo, a tall slim Nigerian girl, who had seen many big lizards whilst visiting family in Africa, turned to Trevor.

"Are you sure that your lizard is an iguana, Trevor?"

Trevor nodded his head.

"Boy," she said, shaking her head from side to side, "I think you're lying."

"Okay class," said Mrs Townsend, "please put away your things. We have come to the end of another lesson. Good afternoon to you all and I will see you on Friday morning."

"Good afternoon, Mrs Townsend," chorused the whole class.

As promised, on his way home that evening, the vet Mr Hixson, went to check on Hildegarde and her kittens.

He gave them all injections, and told Tom's parents that he would return in four weeks.

"Please keep me informed about this little one's progress," he said turning to Tom, "Not five, but six, eh my boy?" He smiled. "Your parents did a good job with this last kitten, but he is a bit on the small side, and there are concerns about..." He paused. "Let us hope, eh?" he continued cheerfully. "He may surprise us and catch up with the others in no time. I must be off. It has been an unusually long and busy day for a Tuesday."

Leslie walked Mr Hixson to the door, but Tom rushed to open it.

"That's all right I can manage. I'll see myself out. Pollyanna, Leslie, night all."

Mr Hixson opened the front door and walked out into the cold night air towards his big black jeep. Leslie called after him.

"Good night Allen, and thanks again for coming," he said.

Mr Hixson waved and drove off before Tom closed the door. He hugged his parents then busied himself cleaning Hildegarde's bowls ready for her evening food and water.

Chapter Six

Hope

"The skies are clear," said Leslie, stretching his body in the small back garden of the island house they had bought only a few years earlier. "Who is coming out in the boat with me today?" he asked cheerfully, flexing his muscles. Leslie turned his straight face from the glare of the sun and tidied his short brown hair with his fingers. "Brian and Craig are coming, Tom, if that will entice you," he said, smiling.

"No thanks dad," said Tom, sadly. "I think I would like to pass today. I don't feel too well."

"I know son," said Leslie, walking over to him.

Leslie wasn't a tall man. He was of average height and build, and Tom practically squared up to his shoulders as they stood facing each other.

"How can I persuade you to stop worrying over Hildegarde and her kittens?" he asked.

"Not worrying about her *kittens*, dad, her *kitten*. It's only the one kitten that's poorly, the others are fine. Look at them."

A fleeting smile creased the corners of Tom's mouth when he saw five frisky kittens together, until he looked at the sixth kitten lying motionless beside Hildegarde. His expression changed instantly to sadness, even though the sixth kitten had been breathing well since the vet's fourth visit.

"We are all concerned Tom, believe me, and as much as I don't mean to sound selfish or cruel, life must go on. Remember what Craig said, 'Be thankful you have five healthy kittens to care for, and Lady H'. Perhaps it's not such bad advice, at least until we find proper homes for them," said Leslie, seriously.

Two of the kittens raced each other to the door where Tom stood. They latched on to the bottom of his trousers with their claws and began to play with the lace on one of his trainers. Tom smiled warmly and Leslie watched them.

"Perhaps if we left Lady H with her kittens and stopped fussing over them, the little one might surprise us and become strong. I am not saying that we should stop caring."

"I know what you mean dad, but it's hard."

"I know, son. I know it's hard," Leslie replied, fixing Tom's shirt collar.

"I fancy a boat ride dad," said Lucy, sliding down the stairs on her bottom. She giggled as she landed on the wooden floor in the small hallway.

"One of these days my girl, you may just do yourself an injury, and I warn you, you won't get any sympathy from me because it will be your own fault," said Leslie, sternly.

"Perhaps she will be sorry then and stop trying to be like a boy," said Tom, petulantly.

"Okay, Lucy, come along, but first you must change those trainers and wear something warmer. That short-sleeved summer dress isn't suitable for this kind of weather and certainly not for the river. Don't forget to change into your wellies. Come along now. Please be quick. I haven't got all day. Brian and Craig are waiting and Lucy..."

"Yes dad," said Lucy.

"Don't forget your life jacket," said Leslie, walking towards the cleared pathway leading to the boathouse.

"Dad, I don't need it. I am not going on a plane," yelled Lucy, defiantly. "I can swim, I'm a good swimmer."

"I don't care how good a swimmer you are my girl," replied Leslie. "You will put on that jacket or you can stay at home and find something useful to do. Let your mother teach you how to peel potatoes, or better still, how to tidy your room properly."

"Oh!" cried Lucy, stamping her foot. "Fiddlesticks," she muttered under her breath.

"It's either one or the other, Lucy, take it or leave it," said Leslie, glancing back.

Leslie always adopted a serious expression, especially when Lucy asked to go out with him on the boat, because she fidgeted all the time. There was always something of interest she wanted everyone to know about, and at times, she bent right over and played in the water with her fingers.

Tom found that infuriating. He had had second thoughts about going out in the boat, but he was glad he had declined once he heard Lucy was going. Besides, he had a lunch date, which he much preferred.

He sat on the wall outside their back garden and watched his father, Brian, Craig and Lucy, climb into the boat, which was then pushed off by a giant of a man.

"Looks like we have another newcomer to the island," said Tom aloud, staring into the distance, as Leslie and Brian began rowing away from the river bank.

Tom couldn't help laughing when he heard his father's scolding.

"You have started that already, Lucy! It is not too late for us to turn this boat around and let you off!"

Lucy had bent over in the boat and pushed both hands as far as they could go down into the water.

"Really, Lucy," said Craig, "that is a foolish thing to do. Please don't do that while my dad and I are on this boat."

Lucy grinned.

"Is there not going to be any pleasure in this ride because of Lucy's behaviour?" Craig's voice was casual, but his expression was moody. "You are being silly, Lucy, and I for one am not going to help you if you fall in," he warned.

"Who's asking you to?" replied Lucy, cheekily.

"That's enough young lady," warned Leslie. "You need to listen more that's your problem, and you need to start taking certain things more seriously."

"Yes," said Craig, "*you* might not value living, but *I* do, and I am sure my dad does too."

"I most certainly do son," agreed Brian, proudly.

Brian was a much taller version of his son. He was a slender man, and he wore his blond hair just a little tidier than Craig's. He frowned at Lucy.

"A little word from the wise, young miss," he said placidly. "Please don't do that again."

Lucy blushed, pulled her hands in quickly and sat twiddling her fingers on her lap. Craig took over the rowing from his father, and Lucy grinned at him and turned her back towards them. Leslie and Brian began to discuss the newcomer to the island, and once again, unseen by them, Lucy bent over and pushed her hand into the water as deep as it would go. After a few moments, she screamed and pulled her hand out quickly. She stood up, causing the boat to rock and almost capsize.

"What in heaven's name is the matter with you my girl?" yelled Brian. "You are going to cause the death of us today, unless we turn back and put you off."

Leslie took the paddle from Craig, started up the engine and headed back towards the boathouse. Lucy's face was red and her eyes were filled with fear and tears.

"I saw it!" she exclaimed, pointing and looking aghast.

110

"Saw what, you silly girl?" cried Leslie.

"There was a great big long thing in the water, with a great big long mouth and enormous sharp teeth, and it was coming after my hand," she said.

"I don't believe a word you are saying Lucy," said Craig. "If by any chance you are telling the truth, I am sorry it didn't bite your fingers off. It would teach you a lesson you'd never forget."

Craig was all puffed up with rage at Lucy for spoiling his morning.

"It looked like the lizard, the one you and Tom told us one of your classmates has as a pet," she said fearfully.

"Now I know you are lying!" cried Craig. "That lizard is only a baby iguana, no more than five, six inches long."

They all stared at Lucy, shaking their heads.

"An iguana, indeed," said Brian. "Leslie, remind me never again to accept an invitation on this boat with Lucy in it."

"Don't worry Brian," replied Leslie, apologetically, looking at his daughter, "Lucy will not be coming in this boat again until she has shown that she has grown up and stopped these dangerous pranks."

"I am sorry," said Lucy softly, "but doesn't anyone care that I nearly got my hand bitten off?"

No one answered. Leslie turned the steering wheel so that the boat made a U-turn and headed towards the far end of the island and not to the boathouse.

Tom jumped off the wall, shook his head and waved, even though they weren't looking in his direction. Then he walked back into the house.

He remembered what his father had suggested earlier. He did not stop to check on Lady H and her kittens as he normally would have done. Instead, he held his head up and walked straight by them. But then he turned back with a frown.

Three of the kittens were nowhere near their mother, so Tom began to search the living room, and it wasn't until he saw they were safely playing together, jumping up and pulling at the cotton throw that hung over the large sofa, that he breathed a sigh of relief and left the room. He checked to make sure he had not left the door to the back garden open, then ran upstairs to his room.

Hildegarde's sixth kitten was breathing well now, but he was still weaker than the others and not too steady on his feet, and he ate much less. He had not been taken off the danger list yet, not by the family or Mr Hixson.

"I am still concerned about this little one," he said. "I have given him an extra vitamin jab, but he needs to begin to eat up if he is to become as strong as the others."

"I know what you mean Allen," Pollyanna replied, looking in the mirror on the wall facing the front door. She dusted flour from her light brown hair. "We are doing all we can, and Hildegarde is a very caring and protective mother to the kitten now. We don't know why she behaved the way she did towards him. I can only hazard a guess, by saying, she must have been exhausted." Pollyanna frowned, "It can't have been an easy task, pushing out five kittens, one after the other. Perhaps like the rest of us, Lady H was shocked at the same time; a bit like having an unexpected visitor, wouldn't you say Allen?"

"Well, yes." The vet shook his head, "That's a comfort, I suppose. I watched her just now, she made sure the sixth kitten was the closest to her and watched him carefully when he made an effort to walk around or dash after his brothers and sisters. I saw him stumble and roll over. He would not move until his mother came to his rescue. She picked him up with her mouth and carried him back to lie beside her," the vet explained, but he looked perplexed as he let himself out of the house.

"Tom!" called Pollyanna from the bottom of the stairs. "Have you forgotten, you told Carl you would attend Mass with them today? It's Sunday, remember? They are also expecting you for lunch."

"I know mum," replied Tom, heading down the stairs. "I was just changing into my best clothes, but I really don't feel in the mood."

"I know son, and I do understand," she said, hugging him.

Without his spectacles - apart from his straight nose - Tom resembled Pollyanna. She was a slim woman, who at five feet nine inches in bare feet, stood an inch and a half taller than her husband. Her hair was usually pulled back in a ponytail, exposing the outline of her attractive soft, oval-shaped face, with its high cheekbones.

"Go on, it may do you the world of good. Why don't you light a candle for Lady H's kitten? Who knows what might happen when it's coming from such a deep place of love and care."

Pollyanna held her son close to her before she let him go.

"Yes," Tom agreed, looking encouraged, "I'll do that."

"Well, here," said Pollyanna, handing Tom a pound coin, "put this in the box by the water fountain before you light the candle - after the service, mind. Whisper a prayer. Ask Mary and her angels to make Hildegarde's last kitten strong."

Mother and son smiled at each other.

"Thanks mum," said Tom, a little more cheerful, as he walked towards the front door, but before he opened it, he turned back to face his mother.

"Mum," he said.

"What is it darling?" asked Pollyanna. "Forgotten something?"

"No," replied Tom. "It's just that Mrs Townsend, our religious education teacher, she told us about a Goddess called Bastet, who lived in Egypt long ago. She said she was a woman with the head of a domestic cat, and they worshipped her. She also said that Bastet likes to protect women, children and cats."

"And certain women would pray to her, if they wanted to have a baby, so she was also known as the Goddess of fertility," said Pollyanna.

Tom looked amazed.

"So *you* know all about her too!" he exclaimed, staring at his mother.

"Don't look so surprised darling. I do find time to read up on certain things. It's all a myth anyway," she added.

"I was thinking," said Tom, "perhaps I could also ask Bastet to make Lady H's kitten well and strong."

"Yes," replied Pollyanna, "That may not be such a bad idea. Why not, the more the merrier, I say try them all!"

Tom smiled.

"Mum."

"Yes dear," answered Pollyanna, showing interest.

"Mrs Townsend looked over at me the day we all had to give that pet talk, after she took out a statue of Bastet to show the class and..." Tom paused.

"What is it, son?"

"Oh, never mind, I am just being silly."

Tom dismissed his thoughts with the wave of his hand.

"No, please don't say that, nothing you say to me is silly, Tom. What is on your mind, won't you share it with me?" asked Pollyanna.

"Well," said Tom, hesitantly, "she, I mean the teacher, Mrs Townsend, looked just like the stone statue that she placed on the table before us. It's not that she looked like actual stone, but her eyes started to look large and cat-like."

Pollyanna laughed and hugged Tom again.

"Who knows son, she might be related to this Bastet Goddess! They say stranger things have happened in heaven and on this earth. That's why I like to read, and I look and listen for anything."

They laughed together.

"Creepy," said Pollyanna playfully, in a deep voice.

Tom giggled.

"Go on, be off with you, Carl and his family are waiting," she chuckled.

"See you later, mum," said Tom.

"Yes, I will see you later darling," replied Pollyanna, "and try to enjoy lunch and the Mass."

"I will mum. I love Carl's mum's cooking, remember," said Tom. "Bye, mum," he shouted then ran off down the pathway.

Pollyanna stood watching her son until he was out of sight, before she grinned and sighed.

"His teacher, half-woman, half-cat, whatever next?" she muttered.

After Mass that Sunday, Tom whispered to Carl.

"Carl, I nearly forgot, mum suggested that I should light a candle for Hildegarde's last kitten."

"That's a good idea... healing," said Carl. "Over there, let's light one of those," he suggested, pointing to the iron table full of lit and unlit little tea lights.

"Mum said we should say a prayer too," continued Tom.

"A prayer!" exclaimed Carl.

He suddenly realised that he had caught the attention of several people in the church, who stopped what they were doing to look over in their direction. He lowered his voice to a whisper.

"Haven't we said enough Hail Marys for one day?" he teased.

"I was thinking," said Tom, "that we could..."

Carl interrupted.

"Tom, you keep saying *we*. I'll stand beside you, but *you* pray. I don't want to. I have said all the prayers I am going to say in this church today, as well as all the ones Gula and I say at home every day." Carl looked bored. "Besides," he continued, "if you intend to ask for healing, my sister is into all this alternative stuff, and she said that a blue candle is best for that."

Carl and Tom looked around at all the containers of candles.

"There aren't any blue candles, Carl," said Tom.

"Yes, I know, I can see that," teased Carl.

"Tell you what," he continued excitedly, "let's go and ask Father Foley, if he has a blue candle. There he is over there, talking to those people."

Carl pointed to a short, slim, middle-aged man, who was dressed in black trousers and a black shirt. He was wearing a long white robe, which had a large green and gold cross down the middle, at the back and front.

"Hurry, let's catch him before he goes off to the pub," said Carl, walking away.

"To the pub?" whispered Tom, controlling the need to shout.

"Yes, to the pub," replied Carl. "Didn't you know? There is a pub below the church. Most people go there after Mass."

Tom looked at Carl, doubtfully.

"Don't look at me," said Carl, "*we* don't. I mean mum and dad, they don't believe in having a pub below the church. They grumble about it every Sunday, especially mum, she has a right old moan, she goes…"

Carl giggled and Tom joined in.

"Phillip!" said Carl, who could hardly maintain a straight face. "Then my dad, he says, 'Yes Eleanor'," said Carl quietly. "What is it now?" he said, changing his voice again.

"I don't feel comfortable going to that church. Perhaps we should go to St Matthew's."

"Goodness, Eleanor, St Matthew's, St John's, they are all the same to me."

"Then my dad hisses through his teeth," continued Carl, still trying to impersonate his father, "not the pub thing again, we go over this every blessed Sunday."

Carl pulled a face and Tom burst out laughing.

"Well, how do you feel, sitting there listening to a man of the cloth preaching about heaven, hell and purgatory, and how we should live a good life, and at the end he never fails to dash off to the pub?" Carl said. "This is how it is every Sunday and the argument goes on all the way home, until dad agrees with mum. If not, she will not stop complaining. And if dad refuses to listen to her, she turns to us. "What do you think children?"

Tom could no longer contain the loudness of his laughter, which made the boys the centre of attention once more.

Father Foley stood by the door talking. Now and again he gave a sly look at anyone who walked past the collection box without depositing money into it, and at those who couldn't be bothered to dip fingers into the holy water in order to wet their forehead and make the sign of the cross.

Father Foley smiled.

"Come on, Tom," said Carl, tugging at his sleeve, "here's our chance to speak to him."

The boys practically ran over to the Father.

"Hello, are you two altar boys here?" the priest asked cheerfully.

"No, Father," replied Carl. "My friend, Tom, wants to ask you a question."

"Go ahead then, my son."

Tom screwed up his face. He hated anyone other than his parents referring to him as 'son'.

"I was wondering whether you have a blue candle, Sir?" asked Tom, nervously.

"A blue candle you say, well now, and just what would you be wanting a blue candle for my boy?" asked Father Foley, reverting to his Irish accent.

Tom squeezed his fists together behind his back to contain his growing irritation.

"Don't we have enough candles here already?"

"Yes Sir, but you don't have blue, do you Sir?" asked Tom.

"No, I guess not. A *blue* candle you say," said the Father again, playing with his moustache.

"Yes, Father Foley, a *blue* candle," repeated Carl, a little too loud. A few people nearby looked in their direction.

"Tom's kitten is ill, and he wants to light a blue candle for healing," explained Carl.

"I see, well now," said Father Foley, smiling at the two brave youngsters.

"Well then, a bit of advice boys. When you don't have a blue candle, use a white one. White is a neutral colour so it is just as good. The Good Lord hears you with or without the candle anyway."

"Thank you, Father," said Carl, tugging at Tom's sleeve again.

Tom felt frustrated, but said nothing.

The two boys walked back to the quietest corner in the church where many candles were already lit. There were only a few people left in the church, and they were in another far corner muttering their own requests, but Tom distinctly heard one of the women say.

'Mary and sweet gentle Jesus...'

It reminded him of when he was smaller and used to say his prayers at bedtime.

"Wait a minute Carl. *I* want to light the candle. It's *my* pet," he reminded his friend.

Carl stood in silence as Tom pushed his hand into his trouser pocket and took out the pound coin.

"Mum gave it to me," he said, when he saw Carl's inquisitive gaze.

"Good, that's a lot, but go on then, put it into the box," said Carl. He watched and listened as the money fell into the box.

"Clever people," he said.

"What do you mean *clever people*?" asked Tom, frowning.

"Didn't you hear as the money dropped into the box?" asked Carl.

"Hear? What have I missed? What was I supposed to hear?" asked Tom.

"The box is empty. It sounds like only you thought to drop money into it," said Carl.

"So?" snapped Tom.

"I never put money into any of the boxes. Did you see me put any money into the collection basket as they passed it around?" asked Carl.

"No, no you didn't, cheapskate."

They both grinned.

"My dad said the churches are wealthy, and we are just middleclass people. We can't afford to go throwing well-earned money into a collection box to make them even wealthier, when *we* need it."

"Well, it's only a one-off, for Lady H's kitten," Tom reminded Carl.

"Yes, I suppose it's a good thing to do for that cause, but you don't have to pay God to heal the kitten."

"I thought of asking Bastet as well," said Tom.

"Bastet, why would you want to do that?" asked Carl.

"No one prays to Bastet, here or anywhere else for that matter. At least that is what my dad said when I told him about what Mrs Townsend told us in class. Aren't the angels, Jesus and Mary, good enough to ask for help?" Carl sounded solemn.

"I suppose so, but I was just remembering what Mrs Townsend said to us, and when I suggested it to mum, she didn't disagree. Anyway, what harm will it do?"

"None, I suppose," replied Carl. "Ask away. It's your cat, not mine. I don't even know whether my prayers are going to be answered. Mum isn't saying a word to us, and we keep asking, Gula and I, day and night."

"It's the doubting," remarked Tom. "You should have a little faith. That's what my mum said."

"You sound like a preacher," said Carl.

Tom lit the candle, set it back in place, clasped his hands together and closed his eyes. Carl joined him and they both began to whisper their requests. At the end of his prayer, Tom added

"If the story is true about the Goddess Bastet, I am asking you too, lady half-cat, half-woman, please help make Hildegarde's last little kitten strong and healthy. My mum said the more the merrier, amen. Thank you."

Carl glanced around to make sure no one had heard the last part of Tom's prayer, and then added.

"Holy blessed Mary, mother of gentle Jesus meek and mild, if my prayers are reaching you, and the prayers of my sister Gula, answer us by letting mum say we can have one of Tom's kittens, then I will know you hear us, thank you, amen."

Carl nodded, and made the quickest sign of the cross imaginable. He grabbed his jacket off the bench and left the church so fast that poor Tom could hardly keep up with him.

That Sunday afternoon after lunch, Tom stayed for an extra hour with Carl and Gula, to devise a plan that they thought might help to persuade Eleanor, their mother, to let them have a pet kitten.

Carl's dad didn't mind. He liked pets, although he said he would much prefer a little puppy. He'd suggested having a puppy to Eleanor, but her reaction hadn't been great.

"If you bring a puppy into this house for the children, who is going to clean up after it and take it for walks and runs?"

Phillip and the children had looked at her.

"Don't look at me!" exclaimed Eleanor. "I certainly will not be doing anything for a dog."

That had been the end of any talk about dogs. For one thing, Phillip, a social worker, was out most days until quite late, and the children would rather have had a kitten anyway.

As for Eleanor, she wouldn't go near a dog or a cat. It was sad really because she had loved the black dog her grandma bought her when she was little – that is until someone poisoned him. As for having a cat, it wasn't that Eleanor had always hated cats. She used to say, 'They are quite cuddly little things', until the terrifying experience that had haunted her for so many years.

True to her word, whenever Eleanor saw a cat, she crossed the road, watching it until it was out of sight. She would sweat with anxiety as her bad memories were stirred, bringing back that frightening August day. So for

127

Eleanor to allow her children to take one of Tom's kittens home, would truly be a miracle.

Chapter Seven

Hands of Light

Tom had suggested that his parents should invite Carl and his family home for tea on Saturday afternoon, when they planned to introduce the kittens gently to Eleanor. After agreeing it with his parents, Tom asked Pollyanna to write the invitation, which he took with him to school on the Tuesday morning.

He handed the sealed envelope to Carl after school.

"Don't lose that now," said Tom, "and don't forget to give it to your mum today. Remember, you getting a kitten, depends on that letter."

Tom pointed to the envelope before Carl pushed it into his coat pocket.

"Is that pocket deep enough?" asked Tom. "You don't want to lose it on the way home either."

Carl nodded. He pushed his hand into his coat pocket again to make sure the pocket was deep enough.

"The letter is safe Tom, don't worry," Carl assured him. "It can't go any deeper." Carl even crossed his heart. "I will give it to mum even before I change out of my school clothes," he shouted his promise to his friend as he waved goodbye and rode off in the direction of his home.

Carl opened the front door and called out.

"Mum, where are you? I'm home and I have a letter for you."

"Bring it here," replied Eleanor, "and it had better not be any problem at school or your father can deal with it."

"*Me,* mum?" asked Carl as he walked up to her in the conservatory where she stood ironing, and handed her the envelope whilst kissing his mother on the cheek. "When have I ever been in trouble at school mum? You know that's not me mum, I don't *make* trouble," he said earnestly.

"I know son, let's see," said Eleanor, smiling. "On second thoughts, here..."

She gave the letter back to Carl.

"You open it and read it to me."

Eleanor planted a kiss on Carl's cheek as he took out the note and began to read.

"Me!" Eleanor exclaimed, "Goodness gracious me! I am invited to Tom's home for tea, with all those cats and kittens in that house. I don't know son, I really don't think so," she shook her head. "I might have to make some excuse, but you, dad and your sister can go along. I'll stay here. I don't want to have to face any cats, not on Saturday or any other day."

"But, mum!" cried Carl.

Eleanor stood the iron up on the ironing board and looked at Carl's disappointed face, her eyes widening.

"I will have to think about it," she said.

"Good mum," said Carl, feeling happier. He left the room, shouting from halfway up the stairs: "Just going up to change my school clothes, mum."

Eleanor did not respond.

"Mum, shall I bring you a cold drink, or shall I come and help you with the ironing?" he asked.

"You, help me with the ironing? What do you know about ironing?" scoffed Eleanor.

"You can teach me, can't you mum?"

"I suppose I could, but not today. It's time to start dinner. Some other time, that is if you are still keen to learn."

"All right mummy, but how about that drink?"

"I wouldn't say no to a cool glass of water. Ironing is thirsty business and I have been doing this for the past hour," said Eleanor.

"One glass of water coming up for the nicest mum in the world," said Carl.

Saturday afternoon came. Eleanor did not accompany Phillip and the children to Tom's for tea because she had deliberately made an appointment elsewhere.

"Sorry children, I had a prior engagement that I forgot about. If I don't attend I'll have to pay," she explained.

Gula had overheard her mother speaking on the phone, so feeling disappointed, they left for Tom's house with their father, Phillip.

Four of the kittens lay curled up beside their mother, Hildegarde, the other two were play-fighting and attempting to climb up the curtains. Gula and Carl grew excited at the sight of them.

"Please, can I hold one? Can I pick one up, Tom?" asked Gula.

Tom looked at his parents, who stood observing with smiles on their faces.

"I don't see why not," said Pollyanna. "Go ahead Gula."

Gula bent down and picked up one of the two kittens. Tom looked at Hildegarde, with the four kittens curled up together beside her.

"I didn't want to disturb her," said Gula. "I don't think Hildegarde would like it if I picked up one of the kittens nearest to her."

"You are right Gula," said Leslie. "Sometimes mothers don't like strangers picking up their young ones."

Tom picked up one of the kittens and joined Gula and Carl. Carl looked at Hildegarde again.

"If mum will let me, I would like that one please, Tom."

"Which one?" asked Tom.

"That one there, the smallest, he is closest to his mother," said Carl. "He looks just like Hildegarde. That's the kitten I would like."

"The tabby? He is the kitten I prayed for in church last Sunday - the one that is still weak and hardly eats."

Tom looked sad.

"He won't die," said Carl, remembering the experience in his back garden. "He will live and grow big and strong, just like his mother. Can I hold him?" he asked.

Tom picked up the feeble-looking kitten and handed him to Carl.

"Let me hold him," said Gula. "Here, you hold this one and I will hold Hildegarde the Second."

Leslie and Phillip laughed.

"That's a good name," joked Phillip.

"It sure is," said Pollyanna.

Tom smiled.

"Hildegarde the Second," said Carl, screwing up his face in disapproval. "His name is not Hildegarde the Second. He will be called Clovis," he said firmly.

Gula sat on a single armchair in one corner of the room, with the kitten snuggled up between her hands.

Pollyanna went off into the dining room to set the table for tea. Leslie and Phillip walked out into the back garden talking together, while Tom and Carl made a fuss of the other kittens. Hildegarde, no doubt grateful for the rest, looked over at them, gave a big wide yawn and headed for her food bowl.

Filled with enthusiasm, Carl looked up at his sister. He knew what Gula was doing, but said nothing. Ten minutes passed and Gula remained speechless, unsmiling and unmoving, her eyes closed.

After a while, Tom noticed flashes of light in the room. To his great surprise, the kitten was bathed in gold and purple light, which was coming from Gula's hands. The light flashed across the door to the garden where Leslie and Phillip stood. They saw the flashes, and so did Carl.

But the boys saw more than the light. There was also a huge figure like the statue that Mrs Townsend had shown them in class. It was Bastet, the Goddess, and she was hovering around Gula. The two friends stared in disbelief, then they heard a voice:

"We are in the heavens and on earth, until the end of time for this earth plane. We will assist those who call to us and deserve our help. At times, even the undeserving may receive help. I am the Goddess of the Ancient ones and my essence is eternal. I heard all your prayers, and have come to answer your request. Tom, trust in Carl's judgement. The kitten he named Clovis, will live. He is no ordinary kitten. You Tom, Carl, his sister Gula, the cat Clovis, and friends, have much work ahead."

There was a brief silence, the two friends stood as if hypnotized, and then the voice began again a little louder than before.

"It will be a time of great adventures. You will all face perils, and experience magic and miracles in order to put an end to negative energies that have surfaced on some parts of the earth. Your journeys will take you far and wide, even to the land of Egypt.

Before that, there is one ever-present enemy whom Clovis must soon defeat. So far, only one person has had contact with him - Eleanor, Carl's mother. This demon is called Mephisto, and at times he adopts the form of a black and white cat. His first mission to stop Eleanor from allowing Clovis into her home has failed. You, Tom, might have a change of heart and become reluctant to give the kitten to Carl, but you must not hesitate. It is a part of his mission."

The gold and purple rays began to fade from the room and from Gula's hands, as the kitten wriggled.

"Did you hear that?" asked Tom.

"What, the voice?" asked Carl. "Yes, I heard her."

Tom was still staring.

"Voice, what voice?" asked Leslie, from the back door.

Phillip shook his head.

"I don't know, Leslie. I didn't hear a thing, unless it was the voices from that passing boat," he said, looking after the speedboat travelling along the river.

Gula opened her eyes and hands, and let go of the kitten, the same little kitten everyone thought would not survive, even the vet, Mr Hixson. The weak one Carl had chosen and named Clovis, because of the order from the voice in the burning bush. The kitten stood up strong on all fours in Gula's lap. She picked him up and gently placed him on the floor.

The family and friends watched as Clovis looked around the room before joining his siblings at play. He was no longer the frail-looking kitten, but was happy, strong and healthy-looking.

"He will be okay now," said Carl. "Give him a little water to drink."

Gula stood still for a moment or two, and Carl looked over at his sister once more, just in time to see the fading image of their religious education teacher, Mrs Townsend. She smiled at Carl, and then her presence vanished with the gold and purple light.

Carl gasped.

Tom stared in shock at his friend.

"Did you see what I just saw?" he asked.

Carl nodded. He did not tell the others who or what he had seen for a split second. He feared no one would believe him, and that he would be laughed at, so he kept his secret. But Tom knew - he had seen her too.

Gula looked over at her brother, then at Tom. She understood what had happened because she had also called for Bastet to heal Clovis, and she believed the Goddess would come. She also knew whom Carl and Tom had seen and heard because she had heard and seen her too, even though her eyes were closed.

Pollyanna returned from the dining room and announced that tea was on the table. When she was given the news, she looked at Clovis. She was filled with joy and amazement.

"What have I been saying for the past four weeks?" she asked. "All it takes is a little faith and lots of love, and who knows what is possible?" She picked Clovis up and kissed him, stroked him gently then placed him on the floor. Leslie and Phillip returned from the garden. They all watched as five of the kittens hurried back to Hildegarde, latched on to her nipples and began to suck vigorously.

Carl, Gula and Tom sat with Clovis on the floor beside them.

"I wonder what's going to happen next?" asked Tom.

"I don't know. What do you think, Gula?" asked Carl.

"I have no idea," Gula replied, "We just have to wait and see."

Sonia Braithwaite:

Sonia's zeal for creative writing was rekindled when she returned to study on a joint BA Honours Degree course at university, in the mid 1990s.

Before that, she worked with children of various ages; in nurseries, schools, and also in a residential care setting, with children who presented challenging behaviour.

Sonia is a trained Assessor, and a professionally trained and qualified counsellor. Before commencing writing her first book for publication, she had been writing extensively since 1995.

www.ingramcontent.com/pod-product-compliance
Lightning Source LLC
Chambersburg PA
CBHW020308150626
46552CB00022B/2200